In Ghost's Den

In Ghost's Den

Manmohan Singh

PARTRIDGE
A Penguin Random House Company

ISBN:	Hardcover	978-1-4828-6816-6
	Softcover	978-1-4828-6817-3
	eBook	978-1-4828-6829-6

Print information available on the last page.

To order additional copies of this book, contact
Partridge India
000 800 10062 62
orders.india@partridgepublishing.com

www.partridgepublishing.com/india

Contents

Fiction

Satire

Adventure

Personalities

Features

Dedication

This book is dedicated to my mother Sheela Devi and wife Renuka who are the main strength behind my life and work.

A Tribute

This work of mine is a tribute to all my teachers who taught me
in my school at Dharampur and at degree college Solan

Fiction

In Ghost's Den

At 2100 hours train reached Badarpur, my destination, a very small station and a beautiful hamlet nestled in the hills of the country's border state and just 20 kilometres from the International border.

A few days back I was transferred to this tiny station as my first posting after my promotion as Sub Inspector. Most of my colleagues in the police department were acquainted with this place and briefed me about its inhabitants and environment. Badarpur was not a crime prone-area. But a few incidents in recent times had rattled the calm of this town.

The case was related to the mysterious deaths of three persons including a foreign national. This man had come to Badarpur to holiday. He wanted to stay in an old bungalow, perhaps built decades back by some Englishmen. Local residents advised him not to stay in that bungalow because for them it was a haunted house. But he was adamant in spending at least one night there. Ignoring the advice of locals he went to stay. He was found dead the next morning. There was no apparent injury mark on the body. The cause of death in the autopsy report was cardiac arrest. Doctors opined that it could have been due to some shock.

The first such death in the house occurred six months back in the same way and autopsy report was not different. Another young man lost his life in the same way only two weeks earlier, and then this foreigner was found dead. Almost everyone believed it to be the handy work of ghosts or supernatural powers. There was panic in the area. What to talk about the general masses, even most of the policemen were reluctant to go there. Under such circumstances I was sent to take charge of this police post. During my journey to the place, my mind was busy in analyzing all the aspects which were brought to my knowledge by my seniors about this case.

"Jai hind sir, I am Head Constable Joginder Singh," this voice brought me back to my present self. One head constable and a constable were standing in front of me. "Jai hind" I replied. "How was your journey sir", was the next question. "It was comfortable," I replied. Then I came to know that the name of the constable accompanying him was Durga Dutt. They both had come to receive me. "Sir, the train was very late today. Generally it reaches around seven or seven thirty, but now it is nine. It is not possible to reach the police station tonight so we will go in the morning," said Joginder. "How far is it," I asked. "About two kilometres," replied Durga Dutt. "Then what's the problem, we can reach in about an hour or so, isn't it," was my next query. "There is no problem but we shall have to cross that bungalow of ghosts. We avoid it even during the day. There is no street light on the way. We shall have to go in darkness," explained Joginder. "So what," I asked. "Sir it is not safe. We can fight humans, animals or reptiles but how can we face ghosts." I knew that at that stage arguing with those two scared souls would have been a futile exercise. Therefore, I asked their plan for the night. Durga Dutt advised us to spend the night in the small waiting room of the railway station and proceed in the early hours next day. Joginder was also reluctant to go. But to me it was sheer stupidity to waste this precious time in a waiting room. But, my guides were almost firm on staying there. Though I could order them to move but taking their mental and physical conditions into consideration I did not oppose the idea of spending the night at the railway station.

It was the month of September, and the weather was pleasant. The waiting room was a bit small but moderately decorated. There was warmth inside. Both brought my luggage to the waiting room and then Durga Dutt brought tea and some snacks. At a tiny place like Badarpur one could not hope for a better supper. The whole night Joginder and Durga narrated the harrowing tales of that bungalow. I did not believe anything, but listened to them very patiently. For me all these stories were nothing more than that of 'an old wives' tale'. Frankly speaking I don't believe in ghosts and wandering souls. I being a student of science have firm faith in my subject, and to me nothing is beyond the realm of science. I was sure that whatever was happening in that bungalow was the handy work of some mischievous elements.

Next morning with the first ray of the sun, we started for the police post. The weather was fine and I was enjoying this nice morning walk. After some distance we reached a trail which lead to our destination. We had not spoken and were enjoying the beauty of nature along the route. Since the path was narrow so we moved in single file with Joginder leading us. After a sharp curve Joginder stopped and pointing towards the left he said, "It is there sir." I followed his finger and saw a huge bungalow. "Is it the same?" I inquired. "Yes," came an instant reply. We were standing hardly 50 meters away from that place for which I had been sent. It was an old structure dexterously designed but now due to want of repair it was in a shabby state. I was excited to go inside there and then, but Joginder and Durga Dutt were reluctant. So I decided to go to the police station first and then to get to the job.

After covering around two kilometres we reached the police post where the arrangement of my stay was also made. After refreshing myself I reported on my duty. First of all I met all the seven policemen including two lady cops posted there. In a causal talks over tea I took note of my colleagues' experience about that bungalow and the people who were found dead there. After our long conversation I did not find anything substantial. I asked Joginder to bring me all the files related to the incidents. I wanted to study what my predecessors were thinking about this problem. On my first day I studied all the files meticulously and jotted down a few important points. The common aspect about the dead persons was that all had gone at night and were all alone at the time of incidence.

Next day I met a few locals including some leaders, businessmen, social workers, students, housewives etc. They were of the view that there were ghosts in that bungalow. The head of the local body Thakur Maha Singh was an influential man. He had contacts with high ups. I met him at his residence. Some other persons like a retired school teacher Mangat Ram,

Forest Contractor Shiv Charan, a doctor Raghuveer Singh and a Patwari Narata Ram were also present. I talked to them about all that happened in that bungalow. Maha Singh said, "Sahib, I many times asked our people not to go near that bungalow. After all how can a person fight with a ghost. First Romesh and then Satnam did not listen to my advice and went to spend night in that bungalow but never returned. We only found their bodies". "Thakur Sahib have you ever visited that bungalow," I asked, "Yes, two- three times but along with some villagers and during the day. I never visited that place alone or at night," replied Thakur. "Who do you think is responsible for all this," was my next question. "Everyone in the area knows that this is the work of ghosts that is why I have instructed all the villagers not to go near that building, so no one goes there. The two persons, who were found dead, were also advised not to go there but they did not believe in the existence of ghosts and other super natural powers, so they went to spend a night there but never returned. In the morning we along with a few constables of your department went in search of them but found their bodies." I asked, "Did you search the whole bungalow, I mean all the rooms and cupboards etc." "Yes, but did not find anything. Both these cases are still pending in the police files". Then I put my question to doctor Raghuveer Singh, "Doctor Sahib you have done the postmortem of all the bodies what is your opinion?" Raghuveer Singh, "We do not do autopsy here it is always done at the district hospital. So I have not done it, but I have read the reports and saw the dead bodies. They all died of cardiac arrest. To me it seems that they all must have seen or felt something very scary or extremely horrifying which stopped there heart beats." "Do you believe in supernatural powers or ghosts," was my next question. Raghuveer Singh thought for a while and then said, "Medical science does not believe in all such fairy tales and so don't I". Though doctor refused to believe in such superstition but his body language was expressing something else. After asking a few other questions I took leave from Thakur and return to the police station. It was time for lunch so I took my meal and again started studying those files. The villagers were aware of the deaths of Romesh and Satnam but they did not know much about an Englishman Roger who was the third victim. Perhaps he did not know the local language and inhabitants of the area did not know English. But in the police records every detail was available.

Next morning I along with some senior members of the staff visited the bungalow. It had a huge iron gate which was not easy to push open. Then there was an almost 50 meter long lawn which was surrounded by long grass and bushes. There was a big porch beyond that and then three steps to the main door. It seemed that this door was not opened for decades. Dust was everywhere. The main door was not locked so we entered very easily. Then took a round of it and tried to observe things but did not find anything which could lead us to some conclusion. So, we came back.

In the evening I called a meeting of the staff and asked them if anybody was prepared to accompanying me to that bungalow during the night. Everyone was stunned. But after some hesitation Joginder, Gurnam, Bansi and a lady head constable Nazleen agreed to go with me. But, Constable Des Raj was repeatedly cautioning us against going there. He seemed fully convinced with the existence of ghosts. I did not pressurize anyone for this duty. I only instructed them to be on alert and come with full weaponry when and where called. We were all equipped with fire arms, flashlights and communication devices. I advised them to remain vigilant and use fire arms judiciously but without any hitch.

Now we were inside the bungalow. We stepped into a big hall. Must be used as a drawing room, because an old sofa set and side tables were lying there. Two big cupboards and two side cabinets were also fixed in the room. We observed everything very minutely. One thing which only Nazleen could notice was the condition of the floor; it looked not in that shabby condition in which the whole building was. Joginder went back to the main door. He noted that whereas the windows had cobwebs, the main door was clean. These two findings were some support to my observation that this was not the work of supernatural powers, because even if such things exist they cannot do cleaning work. The hall was attached with three living rooms. The condition of these rooms was different from the main hall. I presumed that someone sweeps the hall once a while. We did not find anything suspicious except for the almost dustless main hall. We came out and inspected the area around it. During search Joginder found a cigarette case. This seemed not very old. No water marks or traces of dirt were visible on it.

While I was thinking, Nazleen pointed to another empty jute bag. I presumed that the bag might have been used to bring grocery etc. All this cemented my apprehensions about the involvement of some human beings in this whole drama. But even then I had no concrete proof or logic to convince others on this point. On the other hand the members of my team were in a state of 'to be' or 'not to be'. In other words they were in a quandary; logics were against their faith which was very difficult to shun. Logically they were against the theory of ghosts but generations' long faith compels them to think otherwise. After my continuous hammering the ghost phobia had started subsiding in their minds. They started thinking beyond that too. Behind that bungalow there was a thick forest with rocky terrain and according to the locals wild life was in plenty and thus hardly any one goes there. After searching for some more time we returned to police post.

We discussed the next steps. Nazleen was first to endorse my suggestion that we should spend one night in that bungalow, so that we could collect first hand information. I found this young lady very brave and enthusiastic about her work. Joginder, Durga Dutt, Bansi and Puran also gave their consent. But Des Raj again tried to convince us with his ghost theory. I out rightly rejected his suggestions and decided to go there in the night. Des Raj was asked to man the police post with the assistance of two Home Guard volunteers and do the needful in case of any eventuality. I also intimated my district headquarter about our decision of spending night in the bungalow. Superintendent of police Satwinder Singh not only gave me free hand to execute my plans but also assured me of all help I needed. Therefore, with full preparation we decided to spend the next night in the bungalow.

The full moon showed us the path when we started for the bungalow. In the next twenty minutes we reached the place and put two cots in the main hall. Some lamps were lit to lighten up the place. I along with Durga Dutt were to stay in the hall. Joginder and Puran were in the front and Nazleen and Bansi were to guard the rear. I took a last round of the bungalow and also searched all the rooms. I also checked all the windows and doors properly to ensure all were bolted. Satisfying myself we took our meals which we had brought in packets. After that we spent some time chatting. Nothing happened till 2300 hours. Then I asked my men to blow off the lamps but keep their torches ready. There was pin drop silence and the darkness was lit only by the moonlight rays. I could hear the snoring sounds of my companion. There was no movement at all. We all were waiting for something to happen. The time was to pass. I suppose that I might have gone to sleep that is why I could not hear a faint sound which Durga Dutt heard. He murmured in my ear, "Sir, I heard a very faint sound of something." I came to my senses and heard the same sound. I immediately flashed my torch in that direction. But there was no one and no movement noticed. All articles in the room seemed in the same places. Then I rushed outside. I was holding my torch in one hand and revolver in the other. Joginder who was on guard near the front door had seen the torchlight and me. "Did you hear any sound?" I asked him. "No sir," was his reply. By the time Puran had also reached. We went to the rear and found Nazleen trying to look for something with her torch. "What are you looking for?" I asked. "Bansi heard some sound and went towards those bushes but suddenly vanished. His torch is also off. I was going to call you but you came yourself." I immediately asked to switch on the search lights. Within minutes the whole area was illuminated. Bansi was found lying on a rock. I rushed to him, he was unconscious but his pulse was normal and he was breathing heavily. There was no visible injury mark on his body. It was 0230 hours and still a couple of hours to dawn. We were trying to bring Bansi back to his senses by sprinkling water on his face. After a couple of minutes he opened his eyes. He was scared. I gave him water to drink and patted his back. He became somewhat normal after an hour or so. He said that he along with Nazleen was moving together, when he went a little further to answer the call of nature. There he saw a huge silhouette coming out of the forest. It was like a monster having very long hair. I tried to call Nazleen but my voice did not come out and then I lost my senses. I don't know what happened afterwards. On the other hand Nazleen was sure that she did not notice anything unusual. Leaving Bansi with other constables behind, I along with Nazleen and Joginder went inside the jungle, but could not find anything. Due to thick foliage and long trees the place was dark and we could not search any further. So we decided to come the next day. Now Bansi was somewhat normal but the incident had shaken him.

We came back to police post. I did not want to discuss anything at that moment so after informing the district headquarter about the development of the night I went to sleep and asked others also to take rest.

In the afternoon I went to the spot where Bansi had seen the monster. But there was no sign. No foot prints or any evidence. Durga Dutt was scared, he said, "Had this been a human being, we would have got his foot marks." Before I could say anything Nazleen said, "Sir, this is rocky surface so footmarks can be got only after minute examination. I was convinced with her observations. We searched for clues. We went quite deep into the jungle but did not find anything which could help us in solving the matter. But my sixth sense was compelling me to believe that I was on the right track. After looking around for some time, we returned to the post.

In the evening when we were relaxing in the police post some villagers came with Thakur Maha Singh, forest contractor Shiv Charan and a retired teacher Mangat Ram to know about the progress of the case. I told them that very soon we will solve this enigma. "Can you fight the ghosts or you have someone who can do so?" asked Thakur. I laughed it off and told them to wait and watch. I did not want to disclose anything at that juncture; because I knew that there was no ghost around, but someone from their own area was behind that mischief. I simply said, "I am not sure whether it is a ghost or some human but be sure the mystery would be solved very soon." "Please take care of yourself it is very risky," said Thakur in a sympathetic tone. "Who on earth can do such things"? Do you have any suspect," asked Mangat Ram. "It is very difficult to say anything at this point of time but soon everything will be out in the open," I said just to pacify them. In fact at this stage everyone except for my own self was a suspect. And if I was right, the culprit, sensing that police does not believe his ghost story might commit some blunder which could lead to his arrest. I asked them if they had any idea about the culprit or anybody whom they have seen frequently moving around that bungalow or nearby jungle. All thought for some time and replied in the negative. I persuaded them to try to recollect. But could not. Then suddenly Master Mangat Ram came out with a revelation; he told us that he had seen Ganpat and a few of his close acquaintances many times in that area. "Who is this Ganpat?" I asked. "He is a mischievous character who one time was the employee of Thakur Sahib. Now he lives near the temple. He has no family. His parents died years back and he has physical relations with many women but did not marry." They also told me that Ganpat had contacts with some outsiders also, who come, stay with him for a day or two. Shiv Charan at once came to his defence. He said, "Ganpat goes to jungle to work as labourer with the forest department on daily wages, I don't think he can be behind all what has happened." Thakur Maha Singh also echoed the same sentiments. Master Mangat Ram said, "I did not mean that he is the culprit but I have some apprehensions." I thanked them for their cooperation and requested them not to tell anyone about the talks which we had. Then I asked my staff about both, Shiv Charan and Ganpat, and find out if there is a connection between these two guys. There was no official complaint ever registered against Ganpat but his activities were certainly suspicious.

My next destination was the office of the Forest Department. I was sure that those people must have some extra information. In half-an-hour I along with my staff reached the office which was situated on a small hillock. That bungalow was clearly visible from that point. Perhaps this was the highest point in the area. I told Devinder Sharma, the Forest Range Officer, my motive of coming to his office. He was a middle-aged man, moderate in height and physique and wore thick moustaches that added to his personality. After formal introduction I came straight to the point. "Do you think this is the handy work of some supernatural powers or are some humans involved in it?" I asked. I think he did not expect such a straight question from me. He looked confused and could not answer for a few seconds. Then he hurriedly gulped some water and tried to look normal. In stammering words he replied, "What... what... can I say, people say it is the work of ghosts and everyone believes it. We don't take that forest route. Who would put his life in danger, after all we all have our families to support, and moreover it is not our job, it is that of the police." I did not expect such a reply from an officer of the rank of a Range Officer. I stared at his face with some annoyance and said, "I know it is not your job, but in a criminal case where three men have lost their lives, it becomes the duty of every citizen to cooperate in the investigation. And moreover it is

11

not by choice but by compulsion that you answer my questions. I think being a senior government officer you can well understand the gravity of situation. So don't feel offended and answer the questions I put to you. It will be in the best interest of law and of yours also." Even after questioning forest employees at length, nothing substantial emerged. They all express helplessness on seeing anything unusual. None of them was able to add anything to my kitty. But I was sure that they were concealing some vital information. I could not believe that the people, who wander days together in the forest behind the bungalow, had not seen or noticed anything. I was sure that either they themselves were involved or they knew the culprits. I also inspected their roll register and some other records. Then I asked one of my lady constables, Arti Guha to keep an eye on their activities.

My next step was to launch the final assault. For this I planned to have Joginder, Nazleen Puran and Durga Dutt with me. I wanted to spend that night alone in that bungalow and keep all others in the periphery. They all were instructed to remain in pairs. They were told to be alert especially in the rear part as I was apprehensive that if anyone would try to escape he should use the rear portion only. I asked Joginder and his associate to barge into the main hall as soon as they hear a gun shot from inside. In case of emergency, I asked them to use their revolvers without any hitch, and apprehend anyone running out of the building. We all were equipped with torches, candles, match boxes, whistles, search lights and loaded revolvers with some extra ammunition. We also had wireless sets. After taking our meals we set out for our mission. It was 2200 hours. No one was in the lanes or on the muddy roads. We were not using any light. Otherwise the risk of being noticed by someone could jeopardize our whole mission. Within an hour or so we were in the lawns of the bungalow. We were making no sounds. After leaving them, I very slowly entered the hall without making a sound. It was dark but the moonlight through the broken window pans was giving some light, and it took my eyes a few seconds to adjust to the darkness. The cots which we brought the other day were still there. I silently lay down on one cot. My revolver was on my right side and powerful torch on my left. Other equipments were kept along side my bed. There was no moment till 0200 hrs when suddenly I heard some sound like the one I heard that day. This time I did not switch on my torch and remained quite. It appeared as if the largest cupboard in the room was moving to a side. First I thought it as my hallucination or I was dreaming, because I myself vainly had tried to push that cupboard the other day. But now it was moving. I tightened my grip on the butt of the revolver and got ready to face any eventuality. I was ready to shoot. Then a shadow seemed coming out of that cupboard. That silhouette was matching the huge body described by Bansi Lal. Then slowly it started moving towards my cot. In no time it was standing at my feet. Then it stretched its long arms and gradually put its palms on my feet and tried to dig its nails in. My heart beat increased. I was on the verge of cracking the case of the murders of three innocent men. Without wasting any time I took out my revolver and fired at the shadow. With a moan a huge body fell on the floor with a thud. In no time Joginder and Nazleen entered the room. I ordered Nazleen to look out and shoot who so ever she sees trying to escape. In the meantime Joginder switched on both the torches to illuminate the spot. Then I heard two gun shots from the rear. I left Joginder and rushed outside to find two men on their knees. They were trying to escape under the cover of darkness but Nazleen intercepted them and when they tried to attack her she shot them on the legs. Both were taken into custody. Joginder sent a wireless message to the police post and asked them to come with an ambulance.

Then I along with Joginder and Nazleen went inside to inspect the spot. First I focused the light on the body of the man lying dead. My .32 mm bullet had pierced through the heart of that man. The deceased had a scary face, long hair and nails. But later we found that his hair and nails were artificial and his face was painted to make it look scary. Meanwhile, Joginder and Nazleen inspected that cupboard from where that man had appeared. There they found a small tunnel behind the cupboard. We entered into it and reached in a well concealed basement. There were sounds of iron chains as if someone was tied there. I flashed my torch in that direction and found one European lady with scanty cloths clinging to her body. She was tied with chains. I asked Nazleen to removed her shackles, gave her water from the bottles kept there. Nazleen gave her a bed sheet to cover her body. In the search operation which lasted for more than two hours, a large amount of contrabands and narcotics were seized. Another opening from the basement was traced to the deep forest. During our search the other day we went very near to that opening but could not locate it as it was hidden in foliage. These people were using this route to bring narcotics from the neighbouring country, and to keep away the locals the stories of ghosts were spread.

That European lady whose name was Julia narrated the whole story. She said, "This bungalow belongs to us. The man you killed was our domestic help. My father had great faith in him. When we left India and went to London, and made him the caretaker of this property. We used to visit this place occasionally. Last year when we came here, it was night and raining heavily, so no one saw us coming. At night this man killed my old father and made me his hostage. He wanted me to sign some papers which I refused to do. Then he started torturing and raping me. For the outside world we were at London. In the village he spread this rumour that some ghosts are in the bungalow that is why he himself does not go to the bungalow. But every night he would come from the back door and spend some time with me. He also used to bring some eatables for me. The three persons who came to stay in the hall died of heart attack seeing his scary face and outfit. He on many occasions threatened to kill me but did not do so because he thought one day I shall sign his documents. Then some outsiders also started to come. They would bring some smuggled contrabands and narcotics from neighbouring country and use this basement as store. Today also two persons came here and left the place just before your arrival."

For me the main accuse was dead and two were injured. Before the arrival of the ambulance I interrogated the injured persons. They revealed the name of the dead and the leaders of the gang. This revelation frankly dazed us. Though everyone was a suspect in my eyes but the names cropped up were unexpected. Dawn was almost upon us, and I had to apprehend the main culprits before they fled. Till now no one except our team knew what had happened, but the main villains would also come to know and obviously try to flee. After giving necessary instructions to Joginder I rushed to the villa of Thakur Maha Singh and woke him up. He was stunned. I said, "Thakur Sahib I am sorry to bother you at these early hours but the matter is urgent and serious. Please accompany us we have to catch the main culprits red handed and I want you to be our main witness". He could not understand much but came with us. On the way I did not tell him anything. He also did not ask any question and sat mum. Very soon we reached the spot and found two human shadows with some packets lying on the ground. Seeing the lights of the jeep they tried to run but I fired in the air and shouted, "Don't move or I shall shoot." They stopped there and then. I asked Thakur Maha Singh, "Come forward and see the real faces of your ghosts." I pointed the torch on their faces. Now Thakur Maha Singh yelled, "You Shiv Charan and Devinder Sharma. It is you who were behind all that. You should be ashamed of your act." I said, "Yes they both are kingpin of this whole act. They used Ganpat as a tool who himself was after the bungalow, but he was not intelligent enough to plan things. On the other hand this contractor along with this corrupt officer hatched a conspiracy because they also needed a place where they could store and conceal the contrabands which they got from our neighbouring country. To keep the general public away they concocted the stories of ghosts. The man who was playing the role of the ghost was Ganpat who is dead in the mortuary." By the time some villagers also gathered.

"How did you come to know about these people?" Asked Thakur Maha Singh. "Two men of their gang got injured and are in our custody, they disclosed the names of these culprits. They also told us that today a deal was going to be finalized but they did not know the exact place. This information I got from my lady constable Arti Guha who was on duty and watching the activities of Devinder Sharma who was one of my main suspects. Tonight she followed him from his residence and informed me on wireless. Rest you know. "Was I also a suspect in this case?" asked Thakur Maha Singh. "Yes, off course you were." Thakur Maha Singh grinned and then embraced me saying, "You are fantastic!" I thanked him and asked him to come to the post to fulfil some formalities. Then I informed our Superintendent of Police Satwinder Singh. He congratulated me and our whole team.

A few days later Thakur Maha Singh and the village Panchayat organized a function to felicitate us. Satwinder Singh recommended our names for different awards. In the evening I thanked all my colleagues especially Lady Head constable Nazleen and Constable Arti Guha for their excellent and courageous act.

I remained there for three years then got transferred.

With the passage of time I forgot this whole incident. But five-six years later, one fine morning, I got an invitation card from Badarpur. Thakur Maha Singh had invited me for the marriage of his grand-daughter. It was a pleasant surprise. It took me down memory lanes and all the incidents that took place many years back. I happily accepted the invitation and went there. I was in for another pleasant surprise when I saw the marriage ceremony was being solemnized in the same bungalow which then had been converted into a decent hotel by Julia, that European lady whom I had rescued. Thakur Maha Singh, Julia and all villagers welcomed me heartily. I stayed there for three days and came back with the promise to return. They packed my car with gifts when I left them. Now no one in the village believes in ghosts. For them ghosts are alive but in fairy tales only.

The Valorous She

The body was found in a thick forest behind a cluster of tiny plants almost 30 meters away from the main road leading to a wildlife sanctuary. When I, along with, a photographer and dog squad reached the spot, it was 03 O'clock and sun had started descending in the west. That was a remote forest area, so there was very little human activity. Only last month after my promotion as Inspector I took the charge of this police Station and this was the first murder case which I was handling as Station House Officer (SHO).

Deceased was stoutly built young girl of 25 or 26 seemed belonging to some affluent class of society. Her complexion was fair and she stood five feet nine inches. She was in costly attire; white cotton top and light blue jeans. Her top was torn from many places. I could find clear signs of grim scuffle between her and her assailants. A lot of blood was strewn all around, clearly indicating the spot of crime. The apparent cause of death was the injury at the back of her head; to me it could be caused by some heavy blunt article. We did not find any belongings of her. I asked dog squad and constables to search around in jungle if they could find anything which lead us to her identification. The dogs took smell and went till the road but could not move ahead. This was clear that attacker took some conveyance from there. Now we started looking for some prints of tyres. After grueling exercise for an hour or so ultimately, my men imprinted a few impressions of tyres from the spot. Though nothing could be said there and then; it was the job and expertise of forensic scientists to establish the things, but to me it appeared those were of a small commercial vehicle like mini truck or pick up van.

I asked head constable Tarsem Lall to call mortuary van and a team of forensic scientists. In the meantime I informed my superiors about the incident. Superintendent of Police Tejinder Singh instructed me to handle the case carefully as it was a sensitive issue. I assured him that I will catch the culprits very soon. By the time photographer could finished his work, I along with my staff was looking for something which could be a lead in this case. But it was not to be found so easily. There was no doubt that she was sexually assaulted, and resulted scuffle led to her death. But I was in confusion about the motive, whether it was a planned well executed murder or was a freak occurrence in a robbery bid or the plan was to rape her only but to my mind her robust resistance infuriated the culprits resulting in her murder. This all was wandering in my mind as I was waiting for the forensic team. The second point in my mind was whether assailant was known or unknown to her. It was two hours when this body was spotted by a passerby named Rajesh when he went inside the jungle to answer the call of the nature. A team of forensic scientists and ambulance arrived in an hour. They started their work and collected samples from the spot. I requested them to procure the blood report as soon as possible because to me the blood found on the spot could give us some important clues in the case. They assured me that they would try to send the blood samples by hand and report will be available in 10 to 15 days. They completed their task in two hours. After sending the body for postmortem and taking postal address and contact number of Rajesh, I returned to police station.

Next day, my first job was to get the body indentified. Therefore the information of finding a body was flashed with her photograph. Besides, some police personals were sent to all the educational institutions of the city to inquire about it. From age and dress she looked like some young officer or student of any university, or a research scholar. She could be a sports girl also. In the mean time I contacted adjoining police stations to inquire if any missing persons' report of such girl was registered anywhere. But there was no such report registered in any of those police stations.

Next day the body was identified as of Jyotsna Rawat a post graduate student of Government College in the city. She was doing Masters in Defence Studies. Her classmates recognized the photograph. College authorities informed her parents at Chamoli in Utterakhand. It is a far flung area. Therefore in any case they could not have reached here before Sunday which was 48 hours away. In the mean time I met her class fellows in college and roommates in hostel. I took her mobile number from Vaishali and gave it to my staff to get its call details. Lady ASI Navneet Randhawa searched her room but could not find anything. Her mobile phone was missing and so were her purse and clothing. Her roommate Vaishali Benerjee told us that she was to go to her home by morning train that is why she got up very early and left hostel before anyone gets up. The security man on duty confirmed that she left the hostel around 04:30 and she was carrying one bag with her. He said that he asked her to wait till he himself could bring her an auto from the stand. According to him Jyotsna told him that she will take auto herself, as the stand was not very far and she had done so on some previous occasions too.

According to Vaishali, Jyotsna was very brave girl. Nobody in the college could dare to pass her any indecent comment. Three years ago one student of her class Satinder Pal tried to tease her but she gave him a powerful slap across his face that he fell on the ground and could not get up for five minutes. Same was the case of Harikrishan, he was after her but Jyotsna gave him severe beating and he had to flee for his life. After that college authorities took strict action against both the students. But, all this happened three years back. After some time both the boys showed remorse on their conduct and apologized, thereafter things became normal. For the last three years there was no problem. Jyotsna was very hard working and disciplined lass. She was an all-rounder, good in studies and sports as well. I also came to know that she did not have any love affair or boyfriend. Her father was a retired army officer and mother was a homemaker. She had one brother who was studying in Australia. Some teachers and students said the same things about her which Vaishali had already told us. Apparently she had no enmity with anyone. All these findings were further complicating the issue. I wanted to know the motive behind her murder, because if motive is found then usually such mysteries are solved.

Then I started gluing the links. Her train for Dehradun was to leave at 06:17 in the morning. Railway station was almost seven kilometers, so obviously she must have gone to auto stand to hire an auto rickshaw. The distance between her college and auto stand is about half a kilometer. To confirm if she had taken any auto from that stand, I along with my men went there and showing photographs of Jyotsna, asked the auto rickshaw drivers about it. Otherwise also there are very few passengers in the wee hours so it should have not been very difficult for the auto rickshaw drivers to recognize her, provided she had reached the auto rickshaw stand. But no one recognized her photograph, all the drivers present there showed their ignorance. I continued my inquiry next morning too but without any desirable result. I was sure that whatever had happened it happened between college and auto stand, had she reached the stand someone must have seen her. So, this was clear that she did not reach auto stand. What might have happened was the only question which needed an answer. I knew once I got the answer culprit would be in my clutches.

Now I was thinking on two points, one, who picked her up between hostel and auto stand and two, was the person known to her who gave her lift. I was ruling out the possibility of her kidnapping because studying her nature, courage, her body and mental strength, I was not convinced that anyone could take that chance, more over her hostel gate was not very far and in case of any eventuality her cries could have attracted the security guard stationed on the hostel gate and the auto rickshaw drivers on rickshaw stand. Therefore I thought that it was the handy work of some persons known to her. He could be some of her acquaintances or merely a formal relation.

Next day her parents arrived. Mother was inconsolable. They were in great shock. They did not want to believe it. But after sometime they came out a bit of that trauma. I said, "Look Mr. Rawat, what has happened is very bad, we cannot bring her back, but I assure you that I will not spare the culprit. You please let me know all details about her- her nature, her friends, her hobbies, her strength, her weaknesses, every minor detail; this will help me in solving the case". Her father told me everything about her. He also confirmed that Jyotsna was to come home by morning train. One name which caught my eye was Rajinder Rana. He was their neighbour in the village and wanted to marry Jyotsna but she was not interested. Rana was also posted in the city in health department. He tried many times to meet Jyotsna but every time she turned down his request. I decided to interrogate Rana. Before going to meet Rana I made all arrangements so the parents of Jyotsna could take her body to their native village for cremation. The body was handed over to them and by evening they started for their home. I also asked them to come back after performing her last rites.

Then I went to meet Rana. He was getting ready to go to the village to take part in Jyotsna's last rites. I put him some very uncomfortable questions but he was calm and replied with confidence. He admitted that he loved Jyotsna and tried many times to convince her but she always avoided him. He told me that on the day of murder he was out of town to attend some official function. For the time being I let him off for the want of proofs but he was not out of my list of suspects, but still I was to cross check what he told me. Next few days I remained busy in interrogating her teachers, class fellows, college mates and other acquaintances. But nothing came out.

This way fifteen days passed but there was no progress in the case. On top of it there was tremendous pressure on me. My superiors were restless and so was I. Her phone records also did not do much help because her last call was made to her parents a night before her murder. There was no phone call either made or received after that. Then I received the postmortem report which showed the time of the death around 30 hours before the autopsy was conducted. According to these calculations she was murdered around five or six in the morning the previous day. Blood report revealed that the blood found on the spot was of Jyotsna and two other persons. That proved that the assailants were two or more and two were fairly injured in the scuffle. The report of tyre prints showed it as of some mini truck, pick up van or any such vehicle. Therefore my assumption of mini truck or pickup van was correct. This led me to think on other lines. Now I was thinking of the people who had such commercial vehicles. Such vehicles were used by the staff of Wild Life Sanctuary. On inquiring it was found that they had five such vehicles but none of them had gone out on the day of incident. Entry of every outgoing or incoming vehicle was made at the main gate of the sanctuary. So, the possibility of the involvement of their vehicle was very remote. But, still those people were not bailed out; my men were keeping an eye on them. They were also keeping a watch on the adjoining hospitals to find if someone with injuries admitted there. We also checked all OPDs because culprits could go back after taking first aid etc. But all that proved a futile exercise. In no hospital such patient or patients got treatment on the day of crime or next day.

Then, I targeted, mini truck, tempo, and pick up van unions. We searched all their records including their phone records but did not find anything worthwhile. When report confirmed that some middle size vehicle is involved in the crime, I again went to the hostel to meet the guard on duty on that very morning. He told me that he had seen three four vehicles crossing the hostel gate in the direction Joytsna had gone, but did not pay much attention to them. Due to darkness he also could not make out if some commercial vehicle was among them.

I was not been able to do anything even after more than a month has passed. I was in quandary. Joytsna's parents had started pressing the government to hand over the case to crime branch. One day my SP called me and gave me only 72 hours to solve the case or face consequences. I was in tension, what to do? In such a pensive mood I got up from my chair and went to the window of my office to look out side to relax myself, I started enjoying the dexterously created township. Glancing on the gardens and buildings, suddenly I saw a mobile tower just opposite hill top, an idea flashed upon my mind and I called head constable Tarsem Lall and asked him to explore all the phone call records of the tower and the details of the phones which were around the tower at the time of murder. There were more than 10,000 calls between 03:00 to 06:00 in the morning from that tower. Gradually it was squeezed to 1,000. We ignored those numbers which were of some known or identified persons or organizations. Then we zeroed it to 500 calls. Most of these numbers were not of our use. After grueling search we were able to find two numbers which previously were not in the covering area of the tower but entered there at 04:30 AM or earlier and used their phones to receive calls just for ten to fifteen seconds. They again vanished after 06:05 AM. This gave me a smile on my face. I asked the service providers to supply me the addresses of those phone numbers. After half an hour I got the addresses. Now suspects were in my books but still I did not have enough proofs to arrest them. I could not arrest them merely on the bases of their phone locations. It was necessary to obtain their blood samples to match their DNA with that of the blood found on the spot. This could be done after taking them in custody but the chances were if blood samples failed I was to be in hot waters. Then I consulted my seniors and gave the report of the development in the case and revealed my future course of action. They were happy on development in the case. Then I requested my SP to give me some more time to solve the matter as I was on the verge of cracking the case. He agreed and gave me ample time to do the job. So, I thought of a plan and with the help of the college management arranged a blood donation camp in the community centre. No one except for my senior officers was aware of the real motive of that camp. I also ensured that both the suspects would donate their blood. Both the suspects were ex- students of the college so they were contacted through some of their college mates and they donated blood. I with the help of Blood Bank officials took away the pouches of the blood of both the suspects. Now I was waiting for the DNA report. It came after 15 days. Suspects were not aware of anything. They were not worried at all. For them it was a routine blood donation camp. DNA report confirmed my suspicion. I immediately informed my superiors and explained them my future plan.

It was 03:00 in the morning and we in two groups were rushing to Dina Nagar a small town 50 kilometer away from the main city. Exact at 04:00 I was knocking at the door of Joginder Pal a leading transporter of the area. One young man of 27 or 28 opened the door and after seeing us he tried to slam it but I dragged him out. He was Satinder Pal son of Joginder Pal. After putting him in the van I rushed back. Meanwhile another team under ASI Dharam Singh apprehended other suspect Harikrishan from other area of Dina Nagar. Before sun rise both the culprits were behind the bars. I immediately informed my SP and other superiors. In the meantime Joginder Pal visited my police post to get his son released. I narrated him the whole story and told him that I had enough evidence to prosecute Satinder Pal. Then he went back. In the evening I called the first culprit Harikrishan, he was an assistant manger and used to supervise the work. I told him to narrate the whole saga otherwise be ready to face the consequences. I told him that Satinder Pal is the son of a rich man and to save himself he would try to put the whole blame on him. Harikrishan broke down easily and he started weeping. He told us whole incidence which I started recording. He said, "Sir, in college we all three were classmates. Satinder used to tease Joytsna but she never gave him lift. This annoyed him a lot. One day when he crossed his limits she slapped him hard in front of whole college. Satinder took it to his heart and waited for the proper time to take the revenge. By the time we completed our graduation and left the college, but Joytsna took admission in MA in Defence Studies. With the passage of time things subsided and Joytsna forgot everything but Satinder did not; but to normalize the things he went to Joytsna and rendered apology for his conduct. Joytsna took it sportingly and they become friendly. By the time I also joined him as assistant manager. Six months back when Joytsna came out of her hostel to board the train early around 04:00 in the morning Satinder was coming in his pick up van. He stopped and gave her lift. She happily accepted it. Satinder dropped her at railway station. That day he came to know that she goes by this train in the early hours. During their casual talks she told him many personal things. Then he took the contract to paint the college and hostel buildings. Now it was easy for us to keep a track of her movements. When our labour was painting the Table Tennis room in her hostel, I heard her talking to someone on mobile and telling the person on other side that she will catch the train the next day in early hours to go to her native place. I told Satinder about it. Next morning around 03:30 he took me along with him and parked his pick up van 500 meters away from her hostel gate in some dark place, so no one could spot us. It was the place from where we could see the hostel gate clearly. After waiting for an hour around 04:30 we saw her coming out of the gate. When she moved almost 50 meters away from the gate, we started the van. Satinder was on the wheel. Reaching near her he stopped the van, and downing window glass said to her, "Good morning Jyotsna, where are you going so early". "Hi! Satinder good morning, I am going to railway station to catch the train, but what are you doing here at this time"? "I am also going to railway station to pick some material lying there, but first I shall go to Wildlife Sanctuary road to load some fodder for the cattle. If it is convenient, I can drop you at railway station". Jyotsna was a bit reluctant, "But, you will reach late and I might miss my train". "What is the time of your train"? "Quarter past six" she said. "Oh! There is lot of time; I will drop you much before that" said

Satinder. She put her bag in the rear part of the van and climbed from the front window to take the seat next to driver. I followed her. Now she was sitting between Satinder and me. On the way we talked about many things. She was not apprehensive about anything. After going three kilometers on Wildlife Sanctuary road Satinder stopped the vehicle and asked me to come down. I came down and asked Jyotsna to remain sitting and wait for us. She did not say anything but just nodded. We both went inside the jungle and after few minutes just called her on pretext that I was got hurt. She left her mobile in the van and came rushing, though due to darkness she fell down twice on the way but reached to us. "What happened", she asked. "Nothing but something would happen now" Said smiling Satinder. "What you mean" she growl. In the mean while we both caught her firmly. Satinder put a strong slap across her face and said, "This is for the slaps you rained upon me three years back and now I shall take the revenge of my insult in front of so many students". We both started our efforts of overpowering her but she retaliated venomously and hit us with such a force that we both fell on the ground. When we felt that we shall not be able to pin her down then Satinder took out a knife and threatened her to kill. But before Satinder could complete his sentence she pounced upon him and snatched the knife. Now she was attacking us, in scuffle she injured us badly. We both were bleeding I had wounds on my hands and thighs and Satinder had wounds on chest and shoulders. She was furious and moving as she was on a killing spree. We were trying to save ourselves. She was hitting us hard and abusing us like anything. When she threw Satinder on the ground and sat on her chest I tried to snatch knife from her hand but succeeded only in gripping her wrist; now her focus shifted to me. She started grappling with me; Satinder taking the advantage of it got himself free from her clutches and hit her hard on the rear side of her head with a stone lying there. This hit made her to hold her head with both hands and lie on the ground. Gradually her body became motionless. She was dead.

We were scared and in bad condition, so we put her body behind the cluster of trees and ran away. From there we went to Satinder's home and narrated whole story to his father. His father called their family doctor B. D. Sharma and gave us treatment at his home only. When investigation started and police could not find any clue for sometime, we became relaxed and were sure that no one can catch us. When blood donation camp was organized, first we thought of not donating the blood but we did not have the convincing grounds to refuse the donation. Moreover we were not sure whether police had our blood samples or not".

Then I called Satinder, recorded his statement which was no different from that of Harikrishan. After putting them in lock up, I talked to my superiors and gave them complete report. They were relieved of the tension and had a sigh of relief.

I also arrested Satinder's father Joginder Pal and family doctor B. D. Sharma for helping the culprits. The bag and mobile phone of the deceased were recovered from the house of Satinder. The pickup van was traced in the farm house of Harikrishan.

Two mobile towers in a span of very short distance made our task possible, because the hostel and the area of Dina Nagar to which Satinder and Harikrishan belonged, was under one mobile tower whereas the auto stand and beyond it was under another tower. Had it been only one tower things would have been difficult.

Mission 48 hours

It was the case of high profile kidnapping. 20 year old Sadhana, daughter of city's big businessman, Banarsi Dass was kidnapped when she was going to college in her car. The matter was sensitive. Captors demanded Rs 15 Crores for the release of Sadhana. The case was with local police but they could not do anything. So it was transferred to the crime branch. Now it was not only the question of one human life but also the prestige of police was at stake. In this duration Banarsi Dass had received four calls for ransom. In the last call they threatened to kill the girl if the money was not paid within 48 hours. Therefore I was to reach to the kidnappers before the expiry of deadline. The time was short. I took four young officers including one lady of the rank of senior inspector.

The case file revealed that Sadhana left for college in her Toyota at 09:00 in the morning, but never reached there. Her mobile phone got switched off after 20 minutes. Her college is not very far and usually she reaches there in half an hour. Her father got first call for ransom at around 03:00 in the afternoon. Kidnapper demanded 15 Crores and threatened to kill the girl if police was informed. The call was on their land phone. Police tried to locate the call but it was made from a PCO near their house.

First of all I talked to the members of Banarsi Dass's family. In family they had Savitari, wife of Banarsi Dass, Sadhana's elder sister Bhavana, younger brother Rajesh, Banarsi Dass's younger brother Duni Chand, his wife Dulari and two college going sons Ravi and Surinder. It was joint family and there was no problem in them. Bhavna was an intelligent girl doing her masters in Economics. She spent her time mostly in the company of books. Rajesh was in his teens and studying B.A. part one. He has his own friendly circle, but it was confined to college only. Ravi and Surinder both were nice boys and family members had no complaints against any of them. My sixth sense was telling me that someone from the family itself is involved in the crime. Though I had no clue, but the first telephone call which came on their land phone made me apprehensive about it, the land line number was not known to many people. Most of the calls were made or received on mobile phones. How kidnapper knew land line number! It was my concern. Other three calls were received on different mobile numbers, including the cell phone of Savitari, the mother of Sadhana. It was also making my suspicion firm, because Savitari hardly uses her mobile. Her number was not known even to the most of the family members. So, all the ransom calls were made from different PCOs and on different phone numbers. No number was repeated. Kidnapper knew that police will put the phone, on which calls were made, under surveillance. He was taking every step consciously.

I called for the phone records of all the members and scrutinize minutely. It took us hours but nothing could be found. There was no suspicious or alien number. All the numbers belonged to known persons or business associates. Time was running out rapidly and we were still clueless. Then I visited the PCOs from where the calls were made. I found that all were situated at the places were population was scanty and very few residents use those public phones. Now I had to wait for kidnapper's next move. By the time I asked Banarsi Dass to arrange money and put it in a bag given to him for this purpose. This was a transmitter fitted bag which could not be burnt or destroyed anyway. There were some chemicals put in the bag which give a smoke of red colour on burning. These all were precautionary measures. But I was to catch the culprit much before that. The typical qualities of the bag were not even known to Banarsi Dass. I simply asked him to follow my instructions.

I told Banarsi Dass to spend maximum time on phone with the kidnapper when next time he calls him. My plan was to apprehend the culprit when he makes the call. For that policemen in plain clothes were deputed around all the public booths from where previous calls were made. A few policemen in civil dress were also posted just in front of the bungalow of Banarsi Dass. We were keeping an eye on all the members of the family and the movements in near by houses. These neighbours were also under our surveillance net work. This whole drill was very confidential and only known to some top brass officers. In all more than 50 officers and other ranks were put on to the task. Almost 25 hours have passed when the kidnapper made the last call. He had warned Banarsi Dass against involving the police. He threatened him that if police party did not leave soon, they will kill the girl. That made him scared and he told us to leave the premises. I tried in vain to convince him but he was not ready to budge. His family members were also in favour of giving ransom. For them it was a simple and easy way of solving the things. When we all were busy in our work, a police party traced the car of Sadhana in a lake just out side the town. This means that kidnappers took her with them and tried to wipe out the proofs too. But till now nothing concrete had come in our hands. The best way for the police was to apparently leave the premises but follow Banarsi Dass when he goes to handover the money. But, it was a risky proposition. Kidnappers could kill the girl even after taking the money. Girl's safety was my foremost task. I planned to take extreme steps only after taking girl in safety.

After some deliberations with Banarsi Dass and family I took in writing that they did not need police assistance in this case. By doing so my motive was to deceive the captors. I wanted to let him believe that police was withdrawn. Because I knew that someone very near to the family or some family member, was involved in the crime and he or she would inform the kidnappers about this development. This would make him a bit callous and in this callousness he could do something silly, which would put him in our net. Then I asked my men to leave the bungalow and go back to police station. When we reach at some distance I stopped the jeep and asked senior lady inspector Rajani Walia to take two constables with her to keep a watch on Banarsi Dass's bungalow and on all the family members and simultaneously alerted my technical staff and asked them to observe every phone call made from any phone of the house. I knew if someone from the family is involved, he or she would try to contact the kidnaper to tell him about our leaving the bungalow. This way though I had come back to police station but the surveillance on their phones was continuing. Then around 02:50 in the noon I observed a call coming on Banarasi Dass's mobile. It was kidnapper who was fixing the place for taking the ransom. I immediately contacted all my men posted near the PCOs and asked who they saw making the call around 02:50. Only three PCOs were used during that time span. Then I was told by my technical staff that this call was made from the booth just near the shop of Banarsi Dass. I again asked constable posted there, about the person making that call. He told me that only three people made calls from that booth in that period and all three were in there forties. One was a rickshaw puller and other two seemed from upper strata of society. I knew that kidnapper could be anyone of the three. So in no time I got a microphone fitted in all the booths from where kidnapper was making calls, so that any conversation in the booth could be heard by the police team wandering around there. I was sure that kidnapper would make a last call before going to collect ransom. I never tried to contact Banarsi Dass or his family in between.

Now it was the game of nerves. We have to wait for kidnapper's next call. It was 11:00 in the night when kidnapper made the call in which he asked Banarsi Dass to come to a near by park with the money early in the morning at 04:00. Police team posted near the PCO immediately took the man in custody and brought to police station in no time. He was Naresh, an accountant in a firm. This firm was situated near the shop of Banarsi Dass. Naresh broke very soon and revealed the whole story. First of all we raided a godown belonged to the kidnapper and Sadhana was recovered. She was tied with the chair. Her hands, legs and mouth were also tied. We completed this whole exercise in less then an hour. Therefore the master mind of this crime could never know that his plan had flopped. At three in the morning I along with my team reached Banarsi Dass's house. There was some movement in the house. Lights were on. I knew that Banarsi Dass must be preparing to go to handover the money bag to the kidnapper. I rang the bell, after sometime servant opened the door. Banarsi Dass and his wife were getting down from the stairs of their bedroom. They were astonished to see us there. Banarsi Dass was upset. He said, "Why have you come? I asked you people to refrain from my affairs. I am going to pay money for my daughter. We don't want any police interference in it". "It is not your personal matter now. Kidnapper is a criminal and we policemen do not take decisions on whims and fancies of anyone. It is our responsibility to apprehend the culprit." I told him. Banarsi Dass, "but this way you have put my daughter's life in danger. If kidnapper came to know that you are still here he will kill my daughter". "Don't worry Mr. Banarsi Dass Sadhna's safety is our responsibility. Anyhow, where is your brother's family?" I asked. "They must be sleeping. But why are you asking this?" "Is it not something unusual that you are going to meet kidnapper, all of you are awakened, and lights in all of your rooms are on. I rang the bell, the sound of the bell is loud enough to awaken anybody and there is already so much tension in the house, yet they are sleeping? Just call them too". I asked Banarsi Dass. Banarsi was a bit reluctant but on my persuasion he sent his servant to call them. Till now he had no idea that why we had come. Within no time those people came but Duni Chand was not with them. I asked, "Where is Duni Chand?" "Sir he has gone out for some work." His elder son said. "When he went", was my second question. Before he could say something, Banarsi Dass spoke, "But he was here till 11 last night. He did not mention anything about his visit to some other place then". I said, "No problem he will be back soon". Banarsi Dass seemed curious to know the purpose of our untimely visit. In normal circumstances no one goes to anyone's house in such odd hours. I, after reading his face, told him to remain calm and wait for a few minutes more. I also asked him that he had no need to go to kidnapper. He was astounded. He wanted to know what had happened. Before I could answer door bell rang again. I myself opened the door, policemen were standing with Naresh. "You know this man?" I asked Banarsi Dass. "Yes, very well. He is Naresh working with Ram Lall's firm. Their office is just adjoining to our shop" said Banarsi, "but why have you brought him here"? "He had made you all the calls for ransom" I told him. "He kidnapped my daughter? Where is Sadhana?" "No he has not, he is simply a messenger. His job was to follow the instructions the kidnapper was giving him". "Then who kidnapped Sadhana?" he asked. "Just wait, he is also coming" I said. After 10 minutes Duni Chand arrived. He, after looking at me said, "My brother told you to remain away from our family affairs then why have you come here. This can put Sadhana's life in danger. Do you realize the gravity of situation? This can be a catastrophe for our family" he was a bit furious. I calmed him down by showing Naresh Kumar's face. "Oh what he is doing here?" he asked. "He recognize the kidnapper that is why he has been brought here". I told him. "Then take him to kidnapper, why brought him here and bring back our daughter". He said. "Don't be hasty, have patience, no need to worry about Sadhana, because her captor is here among your family members then who is going to harm her." They all were stunned at my revelation. "Who is he!" asked Banarasi. I asked Naresh to disclose his name. "It is Duni Chand" said Naresh. Everyone was in great shock. It was unbelievable. They could not utter a single word for a moment. Duni Chand blasted, "he is telling naked lie. Why should I kidnap my own niece?" I held him from the neck and said, "Where were you the whole night?" "I had gone to do some of my personal works" he tried to evade this question. Banarsi Dass, "Which work you had gone to do, just let me know that"? I asked Banarsi Dass to remain calm and asked Duni Chand, "Look Duni Chand your game is over. Narrate whole saga or I shall have to use my methods, which you may not like." He silently went back and took a chair. "Now start or otherwise my policemen will start their campaign. Yes come on". I roared.

He was completely shaken. Then he asked for a glass of water. After drinking water he started, "Our parents did great injustice to me, they gave whole of their property to Banarsi Dass. I am completely dependent upon him. He questions every penny, I spend on anything. I wanted to take huge amount in cash and let my sons do their own business. For this I planned the kidnapping of Sandhya. We know that she goes alone to college. I hired two men who intercept Sadhana's car before college and on gun point took her away. Her mobile phone was thrown in the lake. Those men blindfolded her and took her to our godown. I knew that you will inform the police. Therefore my hired men used different PCOs for making ransom calls.

Those all goons were hired from different cities so that Sandhya could not recognize them.

After his confession I arrested all the persons involved in the case. I informed my superiors. They appreciated my work and congratulated me for solving the case in stipulated period.

That Night in the Wild

She was wheezing, stumbling, huffing but running. It was the race for life; a little hesitation on her part could part her soul from the body. In that romantic moonlit night where she could have sat below a big tree hand in hand with her lover on the carpet of foliage and let him make love to her, she was rushing to save herself from the on rushing Tusker. This huge animal seemed in no mood to have any kind of mercy on her. She might have annoyed that mighty creature by doing something undesirable. It all was happening in Nilgiri hills the abode of elephants. It is also a well known tourist place where people from all over the world throng for excursion and watch wild animals in their natural habitat. It is always a thrilling and exciting experience to witness these animals in the lap of nature. We were also there for the same reason. Three days passed uneventfully. We just roamed here and there, watched animals in the forest. But it was all a routine exercise, which we enjoyed a lot. Next day was our last day in this resort. We were packing our belongings and planning to say good bye to the people of the resort and especially its owner Savi, who was incidentally my friend, college mate and member of our troupe. It was her persuasion that we were there in her resort. All was well but sometime the most experienced person can commit blunder, as Savi did.

On that fateful day Savi left for forest in the afternoon. I asked her to take some one with her. A mischievous grin came on her beautiful face. "You want to accompany me alone to this secluded place, what is in your mind boss"? She said jokingly. "Then go to hell"!! I said. "Don't worry I will not go alone take you too with me". Then she laughed and went away. I knew her nature she was in a mood to go alone. She also conveyed to her staff that she was not going that far and will be back in an hour or two. But when she did not turn up till 05.30 then we started search for her. Ravi the most experienced man of the whole lot, led us to forest. We divided ourselves in four groups and started combing operation. I along with Rajan had to comb North- East side. There were thick bushes and it was very difficult to make our way. We were moving and calling her. But there was no response. My worry was the lengthening shadows. Light was fading fast. Though those were moon lit nights but moon was to come late. It would have been very difficult to trace her in the dark. I asked Rajan to go back and bring something to light the area and I myself climbed a small hill top. Then all of sudden I saw her run for life. I did not know what would happen but I only knew that the life of Savi was in danger and I was to do something to save her.

Animals particularly elephants don't stand any type of disturbance. It is a moody animal. You can never be sure about its next move. A little wrong judgment on ones part can be suicidal. Savi had spent a long time in different forests so she was well accustomed to the nature of animals. She knew that she cannot beat the pace of the beast, so she was looking for some detour to deceive the animal. I was watching all this helplessly from a safe distance. Though I wanted to help her but could not do much except for making noise and flashing anything in my hands to distract the animal. A little distraction could save the life of Savi, but the chances seemed very remote. I am known for my positivity among my friends, reason being that I never lose hope. I proved it many times during my various trekking expeditions. I might not be wrong if I say that in every such sojourn we had been encountering such situations. I believe that there is always a safe passage in every such situation, but we generally cannot notice it due to nervousness and anxiety. If we think coolly with all our nerves intact some way out can be found. I did so many times in the past. So, generally I am confidant. But this time things were different. I was quite away from the place of occurrence and had nothing in my possession which could scare or distract the animal.

Savi was a daring and an experienced campaigner. I had a long association with her. We had trekked a lot in different parts of the country, I was not apprehensive about her ability to deceive the pachyderm but my only worry was the timing of the event. Would she get enough time to dodge the elephant? The distance between beast and Savi was narrowing down constantly. She was losing her stamina; her pace had started slowing down. The fatigue was appearing on her body. I could not see her face from that distance but presume that she was exhausting. The sun had already gone down so there can be dark any time. This was making her task difficult. On the other hand I was not in a position to render her any help except for disturbing the elephant by making different kind of noises so that she gets time to detour her running track without being noticed by the pachyderm. To me that was the only way to save the dame but chances seemed remote. Anyhow, I was to do something, I could not let her die this way. After all she was my responsibility; I was the leader of the group. And moreover she was my friend and we had known each other from our college days. She was the prettiest and most beautiful gal in the college.

In that situation I had no time for any long term planning. Whatever I was to do it was to be done there and then. Therefore I took a decision and jumped from the place I was sitting on. I was trying to make loud noise and waving my hands above my head. Though I was not sure to which extent it would work but I had no other choice. My voice was loud and echoing in that quiet atmosphere of that forest. Now I was on plain land so was not been able to see what was happening on the other side. But I was sure that Savi was safe and elephant had not trampled her, because neither I heard the shrieks of Savi nor the trumpet of tusker. But I had to rush through the forest at my optimum speed because I did not know how long Savi will be able to dodge that beast. I had to reach her before elephant catches her. Though I am a champion Cross Country runner but this was a different game. My breathlessness and noise certainly distracted the on rushing animal. In few minutes I reached the spot. Tusker was hardly fifty meter away, and Savi was in between me and elephant. Elephant stopped a bit. It might have got my smell or my loud voices distracted the animal. We all three were there. All were standing still, perhaps waiting for others to make first move. I did not know what was going in elephant's mind. Though I am not an expert in elephantine behavior, but I wished that beast should not attack. But, it was still there and staring on us. And all of sudden it started moving towards us. I did not know who his target was, but we both were in danger. We had no choice then to flee. I shouted, "Run Savi run to other side". I tried to attract the beast towards me. Savi took the other way and I ran in opposite direction. But tusker was following her. Her life was in real danger. I could not control my emotions and decided to face the animal from front. I also started running behind the elephant. I tried to hit it with stones but it did not work much. Elephant was not giving any attention to all that. He was behind Savi. This was the area where moon light was obstructed by some big trees. Therefore it was dark there. In that darkness my foot hit a stone and I lost my balance. I don't know where I fell but before I could get up elephant and Savi were out of my sight. But I followed the same path on which they both had gone.

Savi was my college mate I cannot see her dying that way. I think no one can leave any human life in the shadow of death without putting his best efforts, so I continued my efforts and within few minutes I discovered them. Elephant was very close to her. But before I could do anything she herself took a courageous step and threw her body in the near by bushes. The sound and impact of her body stirred the foliage around. These sudden and unexpected movements and sounds put the huge animal in a quandary. It was little confused. This gave valuable time to Savi to crawl towards safety. But Tusker was still looking for her, though he was slow, but still trying to get the smell of its prey. It was inching its way towards her. Tusker was so near to her that she could not breathe even. The scene I saw next compelled me to skip a beat. Elephant was standing exactly on Savi and she was crouching between its front legs. If it takes even half step forward, Savi would go. I was watching it in light of moon and wishing that pachyderm does not move.

It is fact that elephants have weak eye sight. It cannot see very far and very clearly. Elephants compensate this weakness by their smelling and hearing power. An elephant can take smell from few kilometers. The smell travels with the wind and if wind is blowing on opposite direction and prey is much lower as lying or kneeling, then it is very difficult for the beast to smell it. I noticed that wind was in Savi's favour, it was blowing to opposite direction, but still danger was not fully averted. The elephant was just above kneeling Savi. My heart was sinking. Savi had stopped her breathing and elephant was trying to take her smell by raising its trunk high in the air. I was afraid that how long she could remain in that posture and without breathing. Every second was hard to pass. Savi's life was hanging in balance. This was the time when I was to think and act like a commando. But before I could do anything, Ravi, the man called 'Tarzan' by his friends and Savi herself, appeared from no where, at least I did not notice him coming, and struck the pachyderm's tale with a hunter's knife, the huge figure turned viciously at supersonic's pace. Ravi an experienced player of the field was well converse with elephantine nature, preempted this reaction so he saved himself by disappearing in the long grass. This action of Ravi forced the Tusker to return with the same speed with which it had come. As elephant ran to the jungle Savi ran to the Jungle Resorts which was not far away and it was her own property.

I had a sigh of relief. I watched Savi entering the Resort. Then I also made my move. In fact Ravi was in near by forest when all it began. He told me that no human being can run faster than an elephant, but Savi was living in forests for the last 30 years so she knew the tricks to deceive the animals. She was running and deceiving the elephant so she could manage to reach near the resort. In that race she might have covered 500 meters. Ravi saw everything and he was behind us but I could not notice him. His experience and timely intervention saved the life of Savi. In few minutes I too reached Savi, there was no trace of any fright or shock visible on her face. I could not believe that a few minutes back that lady was in real danger of losing her life. "You were really on the door of hell" I said controlling my breath. She gave her old smile and winked her eye, "How I could without you. I told you that I will take you along with me". She gave a loud laughter. A faded smile appeared on my lips too. All others also laughed.

Now five years have passed and we have gone on many adventure trips in between, but the scary scene of that night sometime haunts me, but Savi takes it as a very exiting wild life experience.

Pals

After doing his daily routine work and handing over the keys to Dalip, the shift in charge Zorawar came out of the factory. It was his daily job. Standing at a distance, Sandeep was waiting for him. He quickly tried to cross the road, but a fast driven taxi disrupted his path. He stopped on the edge of the footpath. By the time Sandeep came and put his hand on his shoulder. Zorawar wanted to push that hand away, but could not do so. Disgust had cropped up in his mind for this hand. While crossing road his eyes met that of Sandeep, so could not fling his hand. But, he gently removed Sandeep's hand from his shoulder and before releasing held it softly for some time.

"Zorawar Dada today you take food at my place", Sandeep was inviting him to his residence. Zorawar glanced at Sandeep's face as if he was trying to read between the lines. He had become suspicious about this sudden invitation. A satiric smile appeared on Zorawar's face, as if he was saying, 'want to trap me? But I shall not become your prey'. He became alert as a prey become on the arrival of a hunter.

"No Dada not today. Today I have to take my food with Sardar Sahib", Zorawar politely turned down Sandeep's invitation. It was his fifth day at Kolkata. He had long beard and moustaches that is why Sandeep had addressed him as 'Dada'. Zorawar Singh felt it bad. He asked Sandeep,

"Am I look old to be called 'Dada' (means grandfather in Hindi language)? Sandeep clarified that in Bengal elder brother is called 'Dada' so he is like his elder brother, not an old man. Then both disclosed their age. Interestingly, Zorawar was 22 years of age and Sandeep was of 28 year old. That way Sandeep was older than Zorawar. They both laughed at it and decided that Zorawar would call Sandeep 'Dada' on the basis of age and Sandeep would call Zorawar 'Dada' due to his beard and moustaches.

In the evening Punjabi 'Dada' searched for a 'Dhaba' (eating joint) where some food is available on cheap rates. Bengali 'Dada' took him to the place and introduced him to the owner of that 'Dhaba'. This 'Dhaba' was on the way to his residence, so both used to go together to this 'Dhaba' and spend some time there.

But today when Zorawar did not talk properly, Sandeep asked, "Dada, are you annoyed with me?" "What annoyance, owners of factory have asked me to do some work at their place, so I shall eat there" replied Zorawar. "Okay" said Sandeep and with heavy heart turned other way around. Zorawar started to the residence of the owners of his factory whom every one called 'Sardar Sahib'. "These Bengalis are really dangerous, Sardar Sahib was right" Zorawar was thinking.

It was yesterday only when he came out of factory and as usual Sandeep put his hand on his shoulder, and then he did not feel bad and both the friends happily went to the place where Zorawar used to take his meal. On the way Sandeep was trying to make him familiar with the different places of the city. He was saying, "This road leads to that place and the other one is towards that". They were lost in their conversation when a car stopped just near them. Both the Sardars where on front seat and Narinder was calling him. These Sardars were his childhood pals. They had been playing with Zorawar from their age of infancy. Then he used to call them Nini and Devu but now they had become Narinder Singh and Devinder Singh. All workers of their factory call them 'Chhote' (younger) and Barey (elder) SardarJi, and so was Zorawar. Now he cannot call them Nini and Devu. The difference in economic status had made a big difference. The fact was that now Zorawar was an ordinary worker in their factory.

"Come in the car, we want to discuss something with you" Narinder said. Zorawar opened the rear door and entered the car, now car moved ahead. Everyone was silent. Both the Sardars remained mute till they reached their dexterously build and decorated huge bungalow. Then they made Zorawar comfortable and started conversation. Younger Sardar said, "Zorawar Singh, we want to let you know that we wrote a letter to our father at Mumbai and told him about you. He became very angry and scolded us for not treating you properly like our own family member. Our father instructed us to make all the arrangements of your stay and food. We have committed a mistake we hope that you would not mind it. From today you would take food at our place." He also instructed the servant to cook Zorawar's food daily. "And for your accommodation we shall do something soon. As you see there is not much space here and sometimes guests also come, so for the time being you can put up at servants' quarters, then some better arrangement will be made" Narinder continued his conversation. Zorawar nodded in affirmation. Whatever bad feeling had developed in his mind was gone.

Now Devinder Singh started, "Look Zorawar you are our own man, you are new to this place be careful, these Bangalies are very dangerous. If you see someone quarrelling or fighting never try to intervene otherwise these Bangalies will stop fighting and target you. They are bad people so be careful".

"Is it so?" Zorawar was stunned. He could not believe it. "And one thing more" Devinder continued, "In tram or in bus never sit on the seats reserved for ladies, even if there is no lady in bus. I am telling you because in Punjab there are no seats reserve for ladies you can sit anywhere. "Very strange, no one can sit even if the seat is vacant" Zorawar was frightened. "Yes, one thing more never offer your seat to any lady" Devinder added "otherwise these people will make hell of you" Now Zorawar was really scared. Devinder continued, "Today you were going with that Bangali, be cautious, you are our man that is why telling you all this, otherwise why should we bother. We do not want you to be in any sort of trouble". "But Sandeep doesn't look like such person. He takes me to the different parts of Kolkata, show me good places and more over we go together to my 'Dhaba'" Zorawar said in disbelief.

Younger intervened, "You are not aware, these people do not work therefore they never earn enough money to run their kitchen. To compensate it they adopt other ways. Same is the case with Sandeep, first he will develop friendship with you. Gradually he will take you to his house and introduce you to some ladies in his family, and then blackmail you that you tried to do some bad things with them. This way he will rob your money". Zorawar was very scared. He had developed hatred for all Bangalis. He told both the Sardars that on that very day Sandeep was inviting him to his house. Both the Sardars said, "That is what we were telling you. Beware of these people. In the meantime servant informed that table was laid. They proceeded to the dining hall. For Zorawar it was very pleasant to have delicious meal. He anticipated this type of meal every day. After the supper Narinder said, "Zorawar, we take supper late, don't wait for us, when hungry you can take your food from the servant". Zorawar nodded in affirmation. "Now you go and take rest, you must be feeling sleepy too", said Narinder. When he just took his feet to the door Narinder again said, "In factory also just keep an eye on these Bangali workers. These lethargic chums do not work properly and waste time sitting idle".

Next day he saw a Bangali was exchanging hot words with Devinder Singh. Zorawar thought these whole hot arguments unwarranted. His hatred for Bangalis increased a bit. Now he was convinced that whatever both the Sardars have told him about the character of Bangalis is absolutely correct. These are very quarrelsome creatures.

Therefore, today when Sandeep invited him to his house he became alert and instead of accompanying him he went to the house of Sardars.

He was about to enter the main room of Sardars palace like house when he heard Narinder was rebuking his servant for making Zorawar to dine with them on the dining table. He further instructed his servant that Zorawar is to be given food which is meant for servants. The Nepali servant had a point, he said, "He came with you so I thought he might be some of your close relations". "Okay, but in future give him the food which all the servants have". It was a great shock for Zorawar, he understood everything. Then he entered the room. On seeing him, Narinder said, "It is good that you have come. Do one thing first take your food". "And you"? Zorawar knew but deliberately put this question. "No we will take after sometime and moreover, some guests are coming you will have to go to market to fetch some fruit" said Narinder. Zorawar went to the kitchen and after taking food he brought fruits hiding from the guests, who had arrived when he was out to market and gave them to the servant. He saw many rich people like Narinder and Devinder were present in the drawing room. There were some Bangalis too among those visitors. Zorawar saw all the people present there were giving special regards to a Bangali. He inquired about that Bangali from the servant. Servant told him that the Bangali was the leader of all Bangalis.

While going to his quarter he was thinking that both the Sardars asked him to remain away from Banglis and they themselves are socializing with them. This attitude of Narinder and Devinder made him apprehensive about both the Sardars.

Next day when Zorawar came out of factory gate Sandeep was standing out and waiting for him. But today he did not put his hand on the shoulder of Zorawar. "You must be going to Sardars place, so will not come with me" asked Sandeep. Zorawar remained mum for a moment and then said, "No Dada I shall go with you. I'll take food latter on". "Would you take tea" asked Sandep. Zorawar agreed and they both went to a tea shop. Servant brought two cups of tea and they started sipping it. Sandeep started the conversation, "Zorawar Dada Narinder told me today that you are very dangerous man". These words of Sandeep were unexpected and Zorawar was not prepared to listen it. The cup of tea was in his hand he was stunned and could not move his cup to his lips. "Did not they tell how I am dangerous" Zorawar asked Sandeep. "They were saying that there is an area in Punjab the inhabitant of that area are mostly criminals" replied Sandeep. "But I belong to the same area to which both the Sardars belong" Zorawar was in a state of quandary. He was very annoyed and he told Sandeep everything which both the Sardars had told him about Sandeep and Bangalis. Sandeep laughed and said, "Oh, Punjabi Dada you are also poor like me, what can I take from you and can you take from me". He was still laughing.

"But why that Bangali was fighting with Narinder Singh" asked Zorawar. "Who! that Chatterji! He was trying to make the union of packing staff and management terminated his services, so he was asking for his bonus" replied Sandeep.

After that for long time they both were talking about the working of the union and the rights of working class.

A few days later when both the Sardars were going to club they saw Punjabi 'Dada' and Bangali 'Dada' walking holding their hands along side the road. Sardars slowdown their car near duo and overheard "But Punjabis will not support us" it was the voice of Sandeep. "Don't worry I shall take care of all Punjabis, you go ahead" was saying Zorawar. Sardars press the accelerator and vanished from the scene. Suddenly a smile of attainment appeared on faces of both the 'Dadas'.

(This story is based on an old Punjabi tale written by Amar Singh)

Satire

Yam Raj in dilemma

It is said that every soul changes its apparel after a specific period of time or as we believe, the time allotted to it by Almighty. As a government is replaced by another after five years or a government employee is transferred from one place to another after completing it's tenure at one place. Meaning by soul leaves one body and gets into another. Since there is no 'changing room' for it on this earth therefore it has to go to heaven (or sometime to hell, as case may be), to change its attire. How it goes? Who carries it? It is still a big mystery, because no public or private transport is available for this purpose. I have never heard on any bus stand conductor calling (yelling rather) for passengers for Heaven or Hell. So the means of transport are unknown. It is said that this department lies with Yam Raj who send his Yamdoots to take away the soul of human or animals. Though some rich drunken spoiled brats make the work of Yamdoots easy by crushing 'encroachers' of foot paths under the wheels of their Mercedes, Sedans or Audis, but officially it is the job assigned to 'Yamdoots' only, by doing so they give a helping hand to 'yamdoots'. It is a sort of a social service. Different religious Gurus or Babas tell diverse and dubious sagas about it, which is more confusing than convincing for the people. I am an atheist so I never believed in such things.

My personal experience is very ordinary. One fine morning when I got up, I found myself just in the court of Yam Raj. Then they told me that I was dead and my soul was in front of Yam Raj for settling the debt credit account of my deeds or misdeeds. The whole account was with them. I did not have even the copy of it. By which mode of transport my soul travelled to Yam Lok, I did not know. Surprisingly, my complete profile was already with Chitra Gupta. This gentleman was acting as a 'public prosecutor'. His job is to frame charges against the 'accuse' (soul brought to Yam Raj) and get it the punishment for its 'misdeeds' which it might have committed during his stay on this mortal earth.

I had some other impression about the judicial system of Yam Lok (the world of god of death). But it was no different from what exists on the earth. On top of that, an 'accuse' is not allowed to hire any professional lawyer to defend himself. I lodged my protest and demanded amicus curiae. But it was turned down immediately. Yam Raj ruled that I shall have to defend myself at my own. At this point I asked for the copy of the charge sheet to get myself prepared for my defence and sought an adjournment. But, Chitra Gupta objected to it. He said, "This man is very intelligent and well read, he can 'temper' with the records and bring fake documents. This is a ploy to linger on the hearing of cases. Due to this ploy millions of cases are virtually crawling for decades in the courts on the earth. So Maharaj no adjournment should be allowed". Yam Raj looked at me and asked, "What do you say"? I said, "Maharaj all the allegations leveled against me are erroneous, fake and fraudulent. It is the nature and job of public prosecutors to level such deceitful charges. They are paid for it. They do it on earth too. Sometime even innocent people are sent to gallows on such frivolous charges which no sane brain can believe even. Chitra Gupta is doing the same thing. Maharaj, the latest survey conducted by National Law University students with the help of Law Commission conclude that 'Poor get the gallows, rich mostly get away'". "But he is not a lawyer; he only keeps the account of man's deeds" said Yam Raj. "But who cross checks the accounts, you don't seem to have any Comptroller and Auditor General who can find faults in the account books and rectify them. On earth too all the wrong entries, scams and corruptions have been unearthed by Comptroller and Auditor General. There is every possibility of wrong entry in books. And Maharaj even one wrong entry on the part of your 'accountant' can jeopardize the life and career of an innocent soul like me. Therefore how could you punish a soul on the basis of these erroneous and dubious records? It is not justice. On earth it is said 'justice should not only be done but seen to be done'. First you should streamline your whole system and make it infallible; only then you can do justice to the souls and to your work". Yam Raj was listening to me with full concentration. "But Chitra Gupta is an honest 'man'; he has been doing it for centuries now, and he never committed any mistake". Yam Raj defended Chitra Gupta. I said, "Maharaj I am not raising finger on the honesty of Chitra Gupta, but the possibility of 'human error' (in this case it is 'divine error') cannot be ruled out. An English poet of olden days, Alexander Pope says, "To err is human, and to forgive is divine". This shows that there is always a possibility of an error when human work is assigned even to some 'divine' power. After all he is to keep the records of billion of souls, how a single old man as Chitra Gupta is now, can do so, that too without computer and any assistant. After all Chitra Gupta is fallible, like any other human being".

I continued, "First of all you call tenders for the supply of computer systems. Transparency is must in such purchases otherwise you could be in hot waters; the charges of corruption can be leveled against you. On earth such charges are very common and maximum political leaders face them. It is another issue that hardly anyone of them gets the punishment, because our judicial system is such which believe that 'one hundred criminals may leave scot free but no innocent should be punished'. Anyhow, you purchase good quality hardware and equally good software, and then send Mr. Gupta and a few youngsters to the earth to train them in computer science. You must have a supercomputer with you too, so that you can monitor the things at your own. In human world, on the earth, cheats even hack the computers; to prevent hacking you must have some experts. Those people need to be here with there bodies, souls alone would not serve any purpose. For that you will have to amend your constitution". "But we cannot do that" said Yam Raj. "Why not, when we can amend our constitution, written by erudite people like Baba Sahib Bhim Rao Ambedkar, for more than 250 times till date, then why you can't do it even once. It is needed to give justice to souls. Otherwise your verdicts shall remain challengeable. Therefore

Maharaj, first do the needful and adjourn my case". Chitra Gupta opposed on the ground that this whole process will take very long time, and all souls will have to wait on the door which can cause chaos and in that condition the possibility of stampede cannot be ruled out. Before Yam Raj could say anything I jumped in and suggested that until all the arrangements are made, defer your programme of bringing souls. It can be done later on in amass through any natural or man made catastrophes like Tsunami, huge tremors, hunger, volcanic eruption, or heavy floods. Communal massacres, epidemics and cast based clashes can also help you. Otherwise also we are inviting with proud many multinational companies which are making your task easy by supplying fast food which is not fit for human body. It is a slow process, but deaths are certain. Therefore you need not to worry at all for that.

Yam Raj seemed convinced with my arguments, but said, "Man I am impressed by your pleading but cannot defer the arguments. But I will deliver my judgment after streamlining my system and cross checking the facts from my own sources". Then he asked Chitra Gupta to start the proceedings.

Chitra Gupta started, "Maharaj this man died of hunger". "Is it a crime" was my question. But no body gave an ear to it. "Count his sins in detail" ordered Yam Raj. Chitra Gupta said, "Maharaj he was very cruel to his family." "It is wrong my family was my priority. I remained very kind to them." But Chitra Gupta continued, "Maharaj, he was born poor and remained so throughout his life. He never took bribe or any such money in spite of getting so many opportunities to get it, therefore his family had to suffer and spend life in penury. Maharaj there are number of examples where men born poor but accumulate huge wealth by sources known only to them. Even income tax department could not dig out their source of income". "But he had a treasure of knowledge and education, then how he lived in poverty" asked Yam Raj. "You are right Maharaj he has retired as school teacher. He was very hard working and taught student with great zeal and honesty, but his honesty proved fatal for his colleagues who too had to work hard and could never leave their classes un- attended. This man never gave tuition to anyone; on the contrary he had been wasting his precious time and talent by teaching poor children without charging any fee after school hours. This action of his put the flourishing business of private schools, coaching centers and academies in predicament. All such businessmen are against him and ready to testify against him. There were ample opportunities for him to earn. He was made the in charge of NCC and NSS, but he confined himself only to the meager salary which school was giving him, but never tried to earn some extra money, which others were earning. Therefore his family suffered. Maharaj he had no right to break the norms of society and let his family live in poverty. Therefore he should be sent to Hell.

But I am not sent to hell till date because as per promise made by Yam Raj that no judgment will be passed until all records are digitized and data is fed in computer. Instead of punishing souls Yam Raj is busy in the process of procuring computers. Purchase is very cumbersome process. Now years have passed when I died but Yam Raj is still grappling with red tapism and mood of bureaucrats. I know he will never be able to clear this barrier, because this hurdle can only be surmounted by giving bribe to top boss to clerks, and Yam Raj will never do that. This way no body will die. I befooled Yam Raj, as our worthy leaders befool us daily. This character of our leaders proved a saviour for me.

God's Bad Luck

It was God's bad luck that he met me wandering in the streets of my village. Unfortunately (of course for the God) that was the day when all oil companies raised the prices of petroleum products for the tenth time in ten weeks. Being a journalist of olden days, I was not affected directly by this price rise; because I have no vehicle, the only scooter which I had, departed two years back after giving me a good service for 15 years. Now it is laid to rest in a junkyard. This vehicle had a long history and many sweet and sour memories. After that I could never had enough money to purchase any vehicle not even a moped. Therefore, the rising prices of these products were meaningless for me. And again when there is nothing to cook in the kitchen, the prices of cooking gas also becomes irrelevant. Therefore a person like me was invulnerable to all these things.

Anyhow I was in front of God. It was a narrow lane, so God had no escape route which perhaps he was looking for. I saw him and tried to bring an unsuccessful smile on my face. It was not easy for a person like me, who curses God for his misfortunes the whole day, to present a cordial posture. But I had to do that, because it is taught since my childhood to do so. It is in our culture to welcome a guest with smiling face even if he is your foe. I tried to camouflage my annoyance with smile and asked the God with folded hands, "Prabhu, you are here! I can't believe it! Were you too invited in the meeting of these oil companies"? He immediately became restless and turned his neck from right to left and then left to right in distress; then he took out his hankie, whipped his brow and with shaky hands dragged a cot lying nearby and took his seat. He was very pale and did not seem to be in good mood. Then with in low depressed voice he said, "Who calls me now? I had come only on a routine visit, as IMF has made it mandatory for me". I was shocked and could not utter a word for a moment then asked, "Prabhu how IMF can direct you! Have you also taken some loan from this world body"? "Yes, two million dollars just to repair some old buildings of 'Duaper' and 'Tireta' eras. It has put some conditions for that. Therefore I have to visit this world everyday and see its condition". "So how did you find it" I asked sarcastically. He became sadder. Then he stared at my face and said in repenting tone, "I should not have allowed these multinationals and other big houses to intrude in my realm. But they play their cards so shrewdly that you never doubt their integrity. Their true faces come on the fore when it is too late to do anything. So, now I cannot do anything and bound to work according to their wishes.

A smile came at my face. God was surprised. He said, "Son how can you smile in these circumstances. Does raising prices of grocery not affect you; do you not have any problems?" I said, "Sir, I am a writer I don't bring my agonies on my face. I express them through my pen. As far as prices are concerned, I am immune to all these 'worldly' things because I have been living with half empty stomach for centuries. Though my names were different in different eras but my stomach always remained half empty. I am also known as Munshi Prem Chand, William Blake, Robert Burn, Dhani Ram Chatrik or Nand Lal Noorpuri and by many more names are associated with me, but my plight is same. Epochs changed but not my fate, and the fate of a common man. I am living in paucity, which I have accepted as my fate, so now I do not react to any such thing. You see Prabhu, nowadays our reaction is only confined to 'candle marches' that too if it can attract media. Our media is also very friendly with such people from elite class of society. The 'petty' incidents like baton charge or firing on striking labourers striving for minimum wages, factory workers fighting for their constitutional rights or peasants or suicides by debt ridden farmers, hardly attract media attention. Even in Vayapm scam in which 47 people have so far lost their lives, media is still reeling in 'ifs' and 'buts'. Now a few people might create a ripple 'in a cup' and then go into shell. Then they will 'adjust' accordingly. You have blessed us with a 'great' virtue of adjusting to the circumstances very soon and accept it as our fate.

God was a bit apprehensive; his eyes were focused at me. He looked at me from head to toe, as if he wanted to be sure about what I was telling him. Then he said, "But this is injustice, you must raise your voice." I said, "You are almighty, why are you wandering in the streets like this, why don't you do something? "Son I cannot do anything, my hands are tied. "But you are God. It is firmly believed in this whole world that you can do everything". "But son now the things have changed. I can't do anything at my own; I have to consult my 'colleagues'. Multinationals are doing a lot of good for you people and I have to look after their interests too. I cannot be everywhere so I have created these Capitalists, Monopolists and Multinationals. They have money, they have contacts, and they have resources, so they can serve humanity in a better way. I was shocked. I said, "Prabhu! But we have been hearing for eras that, 'because God cannot be everywhere so he has created mother' how these profit making business tycoons can take mother's place. "You know son, the era has changed and these millionaires have taken over everything even the place of mother, as I have already told you that my hands are tied" answered the God.

My sarcasm came into fore. I said, "Prabhu, your hands are always tied. Those were tied during Mahabharata war and in Ramayana too. Everything happened in front of your eyes but you remained mute spectator. You always look for some excuses even to extricate the worst elements from the earth. One thing I could never understand that why your loyalty and commitment remains with the crown. Why it is not with the peasants toiling day and night in the fields and the labourers sweating in scorching heat in search of a morsel. They have no clothing and no roof".

God had no defence to my salvos. He only said, "I am helpless I cannot annoy the people who have the capacity to spend a lot of money. After all I am to run this world". "Prabhu, tell me whether you are running the world or a 'minority' government". God had no answer to my questions and I too had left with no question for his answers.

Mendacity is an art!

Mendacity is an art. It sounds weird. Doesn't it? You must be thinking what is 'art' in it? We all now and then tell a lie, it is common. It is an old saying that everyone knows how to 'weep' or how to 'sing', so is mendacity. Then what is art in it? In fact art does not lie in telling a lie what it is in how convincingly you tell it. This is also an art that no one catches you when you tell some untrue story. The biggest magic in telling a perfect lie is that even if you are caught, you still win the faith of the people. The people show their sympathies with you; they are convinced that you must have told a lie under some compulsions. Otherwise also, it is an old saying that the lie which saves someone's life or honour is not a lie.

Now the time has come when some coaching classes are required to give professional training to professional lairs. This way their talent can be nurtured. There should be a tough entrance test for admission in this course. Only talented people should be admitted in these courses. There should not be any type of reservation in it. Reservation will bring down the standard of these courses. It is true that we all can tell better lie than the other but talent is talent. A talent can be nurtured but not created. And moreover we can not ignore merit. After all these students are future of the country. Ultimately they are to hold the reins of this great nation today or tomorrow, the nation which has the population of more than 125 crores.

Out of these 125 crores 80 crores earn only less then 20 rupees a day. That makes their task easy. They do not need to worry about these 80 crores. In this era of globalization who cares about such creatures? For us only 45 crores live here. To deal with these 45 crores we need such professionals who can make fool of every common man. Who can tell white lies with such confidence and precision that no body can catch him easily? He should be an expert in making false promises and breaking commitments. Such people have very bright future in politics and corporate world. They need such 'talent' very badly. In coaching classes these students should be taught to work 'shamelessly', they should also be trained for not using their own precious brains but follow the instructions and orders of their bosses because 'Boss is always right'. Such professionals who refrain from using their own brains get lucrative packages. The professionals, who question the boss, find themselves on the road very soon. These owners of big business houses and other bosses are not used to listen anything other than 'yes sir'. This is another thing that the crusader of this system America itself is in hot waters, so are his European friends.

America is grappling with the system they have evolved, but we are feeling proud in adopting the same. We are teaching our wards, how to sell anything, whether it is a product or his self respect. In this corporate world the word like 'self respect' does not exist. For them money is everything. All the executives are given targets and deadlines. To achieve these almost unachievable targets, executives use all sorts of tricks. They lie with everyone, for them achieving any set target is like climbing Mount Everest. But they forget that Mount Everest is only one but their targets are many. There is no end to it. You achieve one and the there is another standing in front. This is the lust for money; this is the lust for power. These politicians and corporate houses are never satisfied. They can tell bundle of lies to earn even a single penny.

On the other hand poor also tell lies, but they tell lie to hide their poverty, they tell lie to earn two time morsel for their kids. They also break law but to get 'Rashan' (Grocery) for their families. They do not sell it in black market or hoard it for profit. They don't see beyond their starvation. But when our democratic government starts catching corrupt officials they will catch a bus conductor, a Patwari (Revenue Officer) or a peon. Then in the court of law they will be equated with coal block scam or common wealth games scam. Is it not the mockery of the system which we have evolved in these long years of independence? But this is life in a country like ours. The system has put us in never ending 'rat race' and we are running at a galloping pace.

Opaque mind is a Treasure

That was the day when I failed in my matriculation examination just for the third time at a trot. To me failures are the pillars of success, but perhaps my family members reacted unmindfully. They were also right, because none of then ever had this great experience of failing in one class for so many times. Beyond my imagination, this became an issue and an 'apple of discord' among members of my family. My mother was the only soul standing by my side. She advocated my case and tried to convince the whole lot about my problems. She told everyone that some teachers had personal grudge against me. My father was furious; he was finding faults in me. A storm of anger, resentment and, despair engulfed the home. I was in quandary that why members of my family were so much upset. For me it was an unnecessary commotion created by some members of my huge family stock, because it was my third attempt only. How a student can get through the examination of none other than matriculation without even failing for two or three times. But no one was ready to listen to my submissions. For them I was a 'villain'. But I was trying to convince them in vain that it was not my mistake but the fault lied with the education system.

Now after so many years when educationists have founded some faults in the entire education system I realize that I was right and victim of wrong policies of the then Ministry of Human Resources and Development. It was also the sign of backwardness. There were no calculators so mathematics was the biggest impediment for me to surmount. Otherwise too, copying in examination hall was a heinous crime in the eyes of law and society, whereas today it is the sign of brilliance, alertness and quick reaction. This talent was suppressed badly in our days. Today not only the candidates but their teachers, parents and friends also go to any extent to provide all sorts of help to the examinees. Some even put their lives in danger in an attempt to provide copying material to the 'erudite' candidates by hanging in windows of the multistoried examination halls. At that height one small jerk can convert a man in to 'history'. They spend lots of money to get the question paper leaked and also trace the paper checker to get their wards good marks. All these 'fundamental facilities' were not available in our times. In those days one had to do whole studies at his own. Dropping out school in those days was a matter of shame but today they equate every school drop out with Thomas Alva Edison. They also say that it is better to became Emperor Akabar by remaining illiterate than to become his ministers by attaining high education.

When I was yelling the foul play in the education system, no one listened to me. Anyhow, after two more 'valiant' attempts I managed to get through my matriculation examination. Ultimately, I somehow managed to do my bachelors in arts in next seven years, proudly in third division. With such a 'bright' academic background I was left with no option than either to join politics or become a journalist. According to my academic records, I had the basic qualification for becoming a politician, but lacked many other qualities which a politician must possess to lead (or mislead) the people. First of all I was bad in using foul and abusive language, I was always scared of using illegal methods and keep harmonious relations with antisocial elements, I was also bad in making fake promises. Though my third division made me a contender for political 'grappling' but at the same time it made me over qualified for the berth in the council of ministers especially for an Education Minister. Though I tried in vain to convince some leaders that I get through all examinations by using unfair means but they did not find any substance in my pleadings. They told me that there are many other graduates hovering around, if they will listen to me then other educated people would also stake their claim, then where these illiterate leaders would go. They said, "you are graduate you might get some opportunities in government jobs but these uneducated people have no way to go. After all they are also citizen of this vast country. No one can deprive them from their livelihood. Therefore this political field is reserve for such elements". That way I was declared unfit for politics. So I had no other choice than to go to journalism. But as my academic career shows, my knowledge of English, Hindi and Punjabi languages was confined only to sending SMS, using Whatsapp, writing letters or applications, but by God's grace some language papers came to my rescue. On the pretext of simplify the language they started adopting the language of 'man of street'. They went further and started using purely 'Tapori' language. For them the grammatically correct and correctly pronounced language was only for 'so called intellectuals' and common masses have nothing to do with the correctness of any language. So, there was no need to keep persons with really good academic background. Therefore, my disqualification became my qualification.

I was gracefully appointed a reporter for collecting news and show the society what happens in it, but practically my job was to bring maximum advertisement for my 'esteemed' newspaper (at least our newspaper management considered it to be 'esteemed'). That way my job turned out to be the job of a 'postman'. Now I started bowing in front of corrupt politicians, bureaucrats, businessmen to get 'alms' for my 'great newspaper'. The newspaper which claimed to be the voice of the down trodden people, virtually worked as mouth piece of rich and influential class of society. Newspapers and TV channels started black outing the news of farmers' suicides, hunger, growing intolerance, communal riots, price rise, victimization of labour class, and rapidly growing unemployment. Instead of that newspapers and channels became the advertizing material for different centers of political and communal leaders. There was an unsigned MoU between these big-wigs and newspaper establishments for protecting the commercial interests of each other. I also became a tool in their hands.

As I have revealed that I am a third class graduate, but to my utter disbelief my editor was a person who could not differentiate between Hindi word 'Saya' and Urdu word 'Shaya'. These two words became the contentious issue between me and my editor. According to his lexicon 'Saya' means 'publication' where as its correct meaning is 'Shadow'. For him there was no word like 'Shaya' in Urdu dialect. Even a third class graduate like me knew that 'Shaya' means 'published'. It was an irony that I was made to work under such a stupid, mindless, and arrogant fellow. So, I was collecting more advertisements than news. Then a day came when on my performance as 'advertisement reporter' I got a very good job in a leading TV channel. Here my work was easier. I did not need to write much. Therefore my intelligence never came to fore. My mistakes in writing and in grammar never surfaced. This was the time when I learned 'real' journalism. I learnt how to oblige politicians, how to make money, how to black mail people and take favour. Then I also came to know that 'unpublished news is more profitable than the published one'.

Now I am a well known and well established journalist. I have received all the awards a journalist can dream of. I have accumulated huge wealth. I am often called to deliver lectures on the ethics of journalism in different universities. I teach them how to remain honest in this profession. I advice them not to take any gift from any one, I ask them to visit my home and find any gift if they can. I know they cannot find one because I say 'NO' to gifts but accept cash only. Now I am an incarnation of honesty and an embodiment of selfless service to the nation.

So my 'third class' fellows don't be depressed in the world of third class people, be a proud associate of this bunch.

Proud donkeys

We are donkeys, and that we are. People linked us with fools. We are synonyms to stupidity, foolishness and un-mindful activities. These petty humans do not understand our anguish. They ridicule us; they make mockery of our innocence, our labour, our efforts and our sincerity. It is great irony that persons who themselves shirk work try to equate hard working and sincere government employees with our community. Since the era of Mahabharata or Ramayana we are like this only. We carry heavy loads. Sometime the weight exceeds our capacity, but we never say 'no'. We know people exploit us, but we do not retaliate or ask for our rights. Perhaps, due to this, we are called 'donkeys'. People do not understand that to bear all this is our compulsion. They think that we are oblivious of our rights; no we are not. We are not humans who do not know their rights. Even If they know, they keep quite. Then what is the difference between two of us. We keep mum due to our weaknesses but human keep mum due his greed because he does not want to annoy any influential man. Then they accuse us of being weak, submissive, foolish and useless. The fact of the matter is that we do not want to disturb the peaceful environment of this country. We are a democratic nation. All have equal rights to live. We don't ask anyone to leave the country or eat what we ourselves like to eat. We also have the right to protest and keep diverse political, economical, or religious views, but we have seen the fate of such people who keep different thoughts from the throne. In olden days they were hanged and today when our constitution gives us right to keep different ideology, some 'open minded, tolerant patriots' either think differently or act differently. To show their patriotism they either throw ink on the persons who dare to show their rebellion or thrash them publically, and those who are 'more open minded, more tolerant or more patriot' even go on killing spree. And then they call us donkey. The things go worse when these crusaders of 'patriotism' start asking people to leave country for eating or wearing differently. Sometime it is done in clear public view in the presence of our disciplined police force. Our police are very sincere to the ruling class. For them human rights mean the rights of big businessmen, bureaucrats, and politicians or those who have the backing of these people. They understand that the people from affluent class are only humans on this earth; rests are inhuman because they live in inhuman conditions. Therefore the duty of the police ends with the protection of these big- wigs only. Our police don't take trouble to register any case unless it has the backing of some influential people of the society. This force is the bunch of obedient recruits. In these conditions when man is not exerting for his rights why we donkeys should involve in any brawl?

We serve the people without differentiating them on the bases of their cast, religion, colour, language or creed. We also serve those whose ideology we do not appreciate. Perhaps thinkers like us today are treated like 'us' by the ruling class. They feel that only 'donkeys' follow rules. They make mockery of our selfless service. In spite of all the prejudices against us we go on serving the people. We don't care what people say to us or about us. It is the bad luck of human race that they make mockery of the sincere animals like us. No one likes to be called a donkey. But most of the human beings possess our qualities. They behave like us, they work like us, they also vote like us, even then they call themselves human and to us 'donkeys'. They would work day and night without asking for over time. These people do not know or have forgotten that thousands of industry workers were shot down on the roads of Chicago by police when they demanded their working hours to be fixed. After long struggle their working hours were fixed, but now most of the humans work nine to twelve hours a day with proud. Even then their job is not secure. Their life is hanging in balance with targets.

The day they miss the shot their job is gone. Is it not ironical that they laugh at us, and call us fool? They don't have courage to fight for their rights and expect us to do that. Their masters pay them less but get their signatures on heavy amounts. These people do not protest. They take it as their fate. For them poverty is the result of their old deeds, some of them relate it with their previous birth. They talk senseless and then call us fools. We donkeys don't laugh on such people but have pity on them.

Adventure

Those 10 Seconds

Seema lost her balance on a snow sheet slope of 45 degree covered with ice like snow and started sliding at a rapid speed, I along with other five of my companions on the trek were spellbound. At that speed she could go in an almost five thousand feet gorge in maximum 15 seconds. You can say those 10seconds was our reaction time. I don't think even a trained commando could do that. We were just watching her helplessly going down to meet her demise.

It was the noon of May 15, 1995 and we a group of 13 trekkers were on our way to Churdhar peak, the highest in Sirmour district of Himachal Pradesh. The sun had started it's descend in the west and sky was clear, which hardly happens at this altitude. The best weather conditions for any trekking expedition. It is a mule tack and the possibility of any mishap was remote. This was my third trip to this mighty peak. So I knew the hazards of the track. To me it is the safest of the tracks on which I had been in Kinnaur, Lahul Sapiti and Pin valley. My first trip to this peak was in July 1986 with three of my friends. That was the time when monsoon was active in these mountains and we all were drench when entered in the inn at our destination. We were shivering with cold and people sitting around fire place accommodated us with generosity. They helped us in drying our clothes, stockings and canvas hunter shoes. But, that shivering was different from that which we all were experiencing while watching one of our friends heading towards an inevitable death. This peak stands at almost 12,000 feet (exact height is 11,796 feet) above sea level. I being the leader was duty bound and responsible for anything that happens on the trek. Therefore the safety of all the trekkers was my responsibility, and I was failing in that miserably.

When all this was happening right in front of me, I suddenly recalled the first words of Mr. Kohli an IB man and the person who introduced me to this adventure. His first lesson consisted of many 'dos and don'ts'. He advised me what to wear and what not to wear, how to walk, where to stay but the most important was- "No track is safe if precautions are not taken. It is the question of life so when ever you go for it, you must go fully prepared and fully equipped with all necessary equipment. A little carelessness on your part even on a safest looking track can cause an irreparable loss". I was so stupid that I did not bring even a rope with me which is the basic need of a trekker. The other blunder which I committed was that I did not enquire from any source about the condition of the snow which had not fully melted and lying in deep curves, and the result of my folly was about to come. I was cursing myself and praying to almighty to save me. I was worried about Seema's parents, how I could face them if she never returns. That was the time when my mind was not thinking about the rescue of Seema but worried about the extraction of her body from the five thousand feet deep gorge. For me she was dead. What else, any human in my position could think in those 10 seconds?

I was recalling those moments when we started from Panchkula on previous day. Seema a born leader was the most enthusiastic member. She was helping others to prepare their luggage and making sure that we leave in time. She was a national level Judoka and had brought many laurels to her state Haryana. Her coach Sudhir Bedi, her team mates Anuradha, Tanver and other top sports persons like Saroj Chouhan an ace Badminton star of Himachal Pradesh who remained unbeatable in her state for eight consecutive years, Raman Arora and Didar Singh, both from Accountant General of Haryana were among the trekkers. We started from Panchkula on our scheduled time. All the youngsters were in jovial mood. Everybody was singing. It is tradition in our group that everyone has to sing individually at least one song whether his or her voice is suitable for singing or not. Smoking and consumption of Liquor is strictly banned. We had reached at Nauradhar a tiny village at the base of the peak on May 14, 1995 by a mini bus courtesy Mr. Ravinder Talwar the then principal of DAV School sector-8 Chandigarh and Badminton coach Mr. Surinder Mahajan, via Parwanoo, Solan and Rajgarh. We spend that night in a PWD rest house.

Next morning was very hot. Nauradhar is warm place so when I asked all the members to carry their woolens along, Seema, Saroj and some others grumbled a bit. For them jackets were a unnecessary weight they had to carry. They could not believe that where we were leading to can be so cold that heavy woolens could be needed. But willingly or unwillingly they agreed to my suggestion. From Nauradhar to Churdhar peak one has to cross three mountain ranges. The starting part of the trek is the most tiring because there is almost two kilometer vertical ascend which is enough to exhaust the trekkers, but once you cross it, then next 10 kilometers become little easy. Then comes the mid way point which is called 'Teesari' in local dialect, means 'third'. It is the place where all routes leading to peak submerge and third range of mountains starts. Due to openness on both sides it is very windy place. Some huts of 'Gujjars' are found here. These nomads come here with their cattle in summers and go back when winter set in. Here my companions experienced first chill of the mountain. Woolens and heavy jackets which were being considered a useless load till now, all of sudden became saviours. In no time all were busy in wearing those 'useless things'. Their haphazard and quick efforts in wearing woolens brought a little smile on my face.

The Churdhar peak was clearly visible from that point. Up till now it was a smooth walk and did not encounter any snow. The real problem started when at very first curve a heap of snow found blocking our path. It was not expected. Anyhow we planned to cross it one by one. I was the first to cross because being a leader and the most experienced amongst all, it was my job. There was nothing to much worried about but with a little carelessness or causal approach one could go to thousands feet down. It was the place where ropes were needed. We managed the things and gradually crossed five such heaps on different places on the way. During this process I found Seema's shoes a bit slippery and cautioned her about it too. I was little apprehensive about Seema therefore asked Raman to help her in crossing the heap. Then we were only half a kilometer away from our goal. It was the last hurdle. I crossed it with some difficulty because with a steep descend it had an elbow curb and slope, and the left side was leading to thousands feet drop. I again cautioned all who were to follow me. Every one except Seema and Raman crossed it successfully. Seema was in front. Raman was at her back holding her hand. There was a stick in other hand of Seema. They both were moving very slow and with great care. Two third of the path was crossed and as I was preparing for clicking a photograph, at that very moment it all happened. Seema made a slip and Raman sensing that he would not be able to hold on 60 kilogram weighing Seema, wisely unlocked her hand and let her slip down, had he not done that the result could have been disastrous. It was very right and timely decision. While going down Seema was making all the efforts to hold anything coming on the way. She was trying to dig the stick in her hand repeatedly in the snow but all in vain. Though, the stick could not stop her slide but changed her direction a bit which ultimately proved a big and decisive factor in her rescue. Her continuous efforts brought her body close to the area where plants had grown. She is a born fighter so she did not want to surrender to death. Her attempts to search for some hold were looking futile but as it is said that luck favours the brave and that proved in front of my eyes. When everything looked lost, a miracle occurred, and a very tiny plant penetrated through the heavy cover of snow came in right hand of Seema which proved the saviour. The plant was cute and beautiful had William Wordsworth seen it, he must have written another Daffodils. I could recall those lines of Daffodils in which he explains the beauty and place where he saw of those flowers. He writes:

"When all at once I saw a crowd,
A host of golden, Daffodils;
Beside the lake, beneath the trees,
Fluttering and dancing in the breeze
Continuous as the stars that shine
And twinkle on the Milky Way,
They stretch in never ending line
Along the margin of a bay.

But now this tiny plant was bearing the 60 kilogram weight of her. She was clinging with that small plant and her ankles were hanging in the air. I did not know how long she could hold on to it or how long that plant could bear the weight of Seema. What was to be done was to be done at once. Fortunately there was a bunch of thick plants on the right. I asked Didar Singh to move down with the help of those plants and hold her hand. It was not easy for him to descend. The safety of Didar was also to be taken care of. He started cautiously taking every step with deep concentration. A little misjudgment on his part could jeopardize everything. But Didar was firm, confident and committed to the task. He knew his responsibility. It took him almost three to four minutes to reach Seema, and those three or four minutes were like three to four hours for us. We, were standing in disbelief, holding our breath and keeping fingers across. By the time Didar reached Seema, it was must for me to assess the mental condition of Seema, so I asked her, "Are you alright, how long you can hold it on"? "I am okey Sir. Let Didar takes his own time" was her response; this gave me a solid hope. Then I saw Didar, holding a bough of a plant with right hand and he grabbed the left hand of Seema with his left hand. This founded the ground for rescue. As I told earlier that we did not have any rope so I planned to make a human chain. I asked Didar not to pull her up as I knew that with one hand it was not possible. In this process Seema might lose her grip. Therefore Didar was only to hold her. Now it was the turn of Raman and Tanwar to go one by one. Though they all three were in the striking distance but it was not easy for them to pull her up, because pulling her up needed one of the three men had to leave branch of the tree and balance himself on the snow without any support. I was not in this favour, but those three did not care for their safety and taking calculative risk, started pulling Seema up. This was the time when we were dangling between hope and despair. I was so tense that in spite of holding camera in my hands I could not click even a single shot; therefore we have no photograph of those heart throbbing moments. In the mean while, Seema's legs touched the solid ground, now she could drag herself too, but those three were on their task. Gradually all the three with one hand each pulled Seema up and after five minutes her feet griped the ground and in another ten minutes she was with us. I again asked her, "How do you feel now"? "Fine as ever" was her reply with a smile on her face. I patted her back and said, "You are fit for Indian Army. Why don't you join it"? "Sure sir I'll do that" she replied. It is coincidence that my words came true, after a year or two she was Second Lieutenant in Indian Army and became Captain latter on. Now she is happily married having a son.

In the realm of elephants

Dusk had just started to descend on Nilgiri forests. The whole ambiance was changing. Birds were returning to their nests. Their melodious chirping was giving a solace to the mind and heart. I was lost in this lovely atmosphere. This was the place where mind feels free from all clutches. It reminded me a few lines of Rabinderanath Tagore which he has written in his well known poem 'Where The Mind Is Without Fear':

'Where the world has not been broken up into fragments
by narrow domestic walls
where words come out from the depth of truth
where tireless striving stretches its arms towards perfection'

He had written these golden words in some other context but in the lap of nature these lines came out automatically of my unconscious mind. But unfortunately I could not rejoice those moments by standing in the heart of jungle because like birds I had also to reach my destination before dark. William Henry Davies has rightly written in his poem 'Leisure':

What is this life if, full of care,
We have no time to stand and stare.

No time to stand beneath the boughs
And stare as long as sheep or cows.
No time to see, when woods we pass,
Where squirrels hide their nuts in grass.

My guide and driver had already told me that we were still 20 kilometers away. This was the Bandipur reserve forest known for elephants. The shadows were lengthening. This was the time when big animals come out in search of food and water. According to an estimate there are more than 5,000 elephants in these forests.

Driven by the urge to see the elephants in their natural habitat and also to meet my old college pal Savita Thakur (now Savita Jain), brought me in those dense forests. Savita owns a beautiful resort named 'Forest Hills Farm and Guest House' located deep in the jungle. The whole atmosphere was quiet, no disturbing sounds anywhere. Most of the guests staying in resort were wildlife lovers. They knew the etiquettes of wild. They all were conversing in hushed voices. I had heard many stories of elephants' aggression; and now I had entered their territory knowing little that all my apprehensions were going to be proved wrong. Savita, who herself had a few miraculous escapes from tuskers, gave me a crash course on elephantine nature. No animal, she said, attacks humans without provocation or fear. In fact they avoid man. There was no reason to disbelieve Savita. After all these jungles have been her habitats too for the last 35 years. Proximity with the elephants has made her a sort of wild life expert. She loves animals and enjoys living with them. She is the first one to build something for wild life lovers and general masses in these forests. There is one dexterously built 'Machan house' and two 'tree houses' to give the visitors a thrilling experience of living amidst the foliage far above and the ground below.

Savita met me very warmly, after all a friend was meeting after college days. During this period 30 summers had passed. My whole fatigue vanished. We talked at length about everything we experienced in our life after passing out from college. We virtually enjoyed the follies of that age again and laughed on everything foolish we did. We also discussed our teachers, our friends, our foes, their traits, and their dressing sense. Savita was excited to show me her whole resort and introduced me to her whole staff. Her most trusted aide was Radhakishan. He was a man from jungle, very smart and fully converse with the etiquettes of forests. After spending some time roaming in the different parts of resort we came back to Savita's place. The darkness had started descending now. The things were becoming hazy. Savita took me and other guests staying in the resort to show some wild life. It was a thrilling moment. Though I am an adventurist but that was of trekking in lower Himalayas or in Shiwalik Hills. Watching animals in their natural habitats was my first experience. Savita took us a few hundred yards away from main resort.

After walking for five or six minutes I found myself standing near 'machan house' built on the branches of a huge tree. Some professional wildlife photographers were stationed on the 'machan house' waiting for the wild animals to appear on the edge of the jungle. They were feeling disturbed with our presence near by. Savita had already instructed us not to make any noticeable movements or flash anything. We were also advised not to wear white or shiny attire. Any shiny object can disturb the animal and make him furious. There was pin drop silence. Excitement was in the air. Savita was completely calm and alert. My fears diminished as I saw Savita standing close by wearing bathroom slippers which indicated that fleeing away will not be required. Soon enough darkness enveloped, only the silhouettes of trees and bushes was visible a bit. A few minutes back we had a rare sight of wild bores fighting for food. But all of sudden I noticed a ripple in the herd of wild bores. They were on the run. Before I could realize what was happening, Savita whispered in my ear-"look straight." I saw the direction she had indicated and spotted a huge figure trundling our way. It was a gigantic tusker, almost 10 feet tall. Its majestic figure was a treat to watch. What a marvelous animal it was with tusks at least six feet long! It was standing just 25 or 30 meters away from us. I was thrilled, excited, mesmerized and scared at the same time. "What if it rushed and trampled us?" But Savita's presence was a great moral support for all of us. She asked us not to panic, watch the animal calmly and admire the majestically built of the pachyderm. It was a great sight. Then slowly it started moving to its right. He would take a few steps and look around; making sure that no one is around before taking another step. We were also moving with him. Gradually tusker changed his direction. Now he was heading towards the backyard of the guest house. We all were following him, slowly and quietly. Savita asked us to watch and enjoy the presence of huge elephant as long as we could. A day before, the same tusker had entered the premises of the resort and damaged one huge dustbin and a few trees. These elephants had damaged one or the other part of the resort so many times before too. But that day when we were watching, it took different route. Though every one of us who were admiring the might of the pachyderm must have watched this fantastic animal many times in circus, zoo or as pet many times but Watching a huge tusker in the wild is a life time experience. We followed him to the distance, but when he started noticing our presence and became a little uneasy, Savita asked us to come back quietly. These tuskers do not want any thing disturbing them. It was a heart throbbing sight.

Savita is a crusader for the cause of the elephants. She wants to remain in these forests and educate people about them. She has earned a great respect in this area. People love her. I felt proud to be her friend. Meeting her after decades was a journey down memory lane. In college she was an innocent but naughty girl. She was a pleasantly beautiful face from a tiny hamlet Hinner of Chail area in Himachal Pradesh. Her transformation into a successful and respected businesswoman deep into the elephant heartland is an amazing story in itself. This leaves a lasting impression on anyone who comes across her. Her love for wildlife seems to have turned her into a most committed and accomplished organizer. I thought as I took leave of my host after spending a day and a night in her august company; and that of her friends in the wild.

Personalities

Final Hours of Bhagat Singh

It was the early hours of 23March, 1931 when Bhagat Singh, Raj Guru and Sukhdev got up. They were to be hanged the very next day. All the three were convicted in Saunders murder case. But with the fear of nationwide unrest against the hanging, government advanced the executions by a day. Therefore instead of March 24 they were hanged in the evening of March 23. In Indian history this is the sole case where hanging has been performed in the evening, otherwise it is always done in the early hours. The whole process of hanging was completed in the presence of officials like Stead, Barker, Roberts, Hardinge, Chopra and deputy jail superintendent Khan Sahib Mohammad Akbar. They all were present inside the jail. The hangman, Massih was called from Shahadra, it is near Lahore. The moment the three revolutionaries were taken out of their cells, they shouted 'Inquilab zindabad' (long live the revolutions).

For the last 84 years we have been remembering these three sons of the soil Bhagat Singh, Rajguru and Sukhdev on every March 23. These three revolutionaries were hanged in Lahore central jail. Whole of the country went in bereavement. People came on streets. The mob frenzy was immense. British government was scared of it. So, they did not hand over their bodies to their families. Instead, jail administration broke the rear wall of the prison and in the darkness of the night, took the bodies to the bank of river

Satluj for cremation. There they cut the bodies into pieces and tried to burn them. But the bodies were half brunt when infuriated mob reached the spot. On seeing the crowd coming on them the policemen ran away leaving behind half burnt bodies. The people gathered on the spot performed the last rites of their heroes. This was not the end of the revolution, but beginning of another one. There was very strong public reaction to this cowardly act of the British government. There are several questions which are still unanswered. These questions are related with the hanging of these martyrs. Our efforts are to find the answers of those questions and know about the persons who helped the British in the execution of Bhagat Singh, Rajguru and Sukhdev, which our government never did even after getting freedom in 1947.

It is a known fact that Bhagat Singh was born at Layallpur (now in Pakistan), and died at Lahore (Pakistan). Many Indian Prime Ministers including Pandit Jawahar Lal Nehru, Inder Kumar Gujral or Atal Bihari Vajpayee visited Pakistan but none paid his visit to any of these two places. Though, Saeeda Deep a social activist of Pakistan, living in Lahore, is fighting to name 'Shadman Chowk' (a place in Lahore where that barrack was situated in which these three revolutionaries were hanged), as 'Bhagat Singh Chowk', but no such effort has ever been made by our own government.

One senior IAS officer RK Kaushik has made good efforts to bring out some hidden facts to the fore. He narrates the final hours of Bhagat Singh. Very few people know what happened on that fateful day. He writes:

"A dust storm swept Lahore on the night of March 22. Justice MV Bhide, ICS, of the Lahore High Court, had earlier rejected the petitions challenging the powers of a special tribunal to issue the death warrants. Thus, the executions became inevitable.

By the time dawn broke on March 23, the storm had settled. Jail officials in the central jail spoke in hushed tones in the room of jail superintendent Major PD Chopra. The Punjab government allowed the last meeting with Bhagat Singh at 10am. Pran Nath Mehta, his lawyer, met him. The moment Mehta left, after receiving four handwritten bunches of papers surreptitiously from Bhagat Singh, a team of officers led by Stead, Barker, Roberts, Hardinge and Chopra met Bhagat Singh. Their unsolicited advice to seek a pardon from the British government was contemptuously rejected by Bhagat Singh. The executions had been advanced by a day and were to take place in the evening of March 23.

The information to Bhagat Singh, Rajguru and Sukhdev was conveyed by senior jail warden Chhattar Singh. A disturbed and grief-stricken Chhattar Singh suggested to Bhagat Singh that he recite the name of god. But Bhagat Singh was busy reading a book on Russian revolutionary Vladimir Ilyich Lenin.

Bhagat Singh had asked a Muslim sweeper, Bebe, to bring food for him in the evening before his execution. Bebe readily accepted the request and promised to bring home-cooked food for him. But because of the security clampdown, Bebe was unable to enter the jail that evening. There was a flurry of activity inside the Lahore jail and outside because authorities feared unrest.

As noon passed and the clock inched towards evening, the district civil and police officers camped outside the jail. They were led by Sheikh Abdul Hamid, additional district magistrate, Lahore; Rai Sahib Lala Nathu Ram, city magistrate; Sudarshan Singh, deputy superintendent of police, Kasur; Amar Singh, deputy superintendent of police (city), Lahore; JR Morris, deputy superintendent of police, headquarters, Lahore; and hundreds of armed policemen.

Pindi Dass Sodhi, secretary, district Congress, Lahore lived near the central jail. The slogans by Bhagat Singh and his comrades were clearly heard at his house. After hearing the shouts of the three men walking to their deaths, the other prisoners joined them in the sloganeering.

Deputy Commissioner AA Lane Roberts was a loquacious officer of the 1909 batch of ICS. When the three young men reached the hanging site, he spoke to Bhagat Singh. Bhagat Singh confidently said that people would soon see and remember how Indian freedom fighters bravely kiss death.

They refused to wear masks over their necks. In fact, Bhagat Singh threw the mask at the district magistrate. Bhagat Singh and his companions hugged each other for the last time, and shouted "down with the British empire".

Massih pulled the lever. Bhagat Singh was the first to hang. He was followed by Rajguru and Sukhdev.

Lt Col JJ Harper Nelson, principal of King Edward's Medical College, Lahore and Lt Col NS Sodhi, civil surgeon, Lahore, were inside the jail at the *time of the executions but did not witness the hangings. After the hangings, the three were confirmed dead by the civil surgeon.*

A huge crowd had gathered outside the jail, but two vehicles led by deputy superintendent of police Kasur Sudarshan Singh and deputy superintendent of police (city) Amar Singh accompanied by three trucks of soldiers of black watch regiment took the bodies and left for the cremation at 10 pm. Sudarshan picked up a Granthi and a priest named Jagdish Acharaj from Kasur and set the bodies on fire outside Ganda Singh Wala village in the night. The bodies were still burning when people from different areas, including Ferozepur, reached there and a ruckus follows".

Kaushik's research reveal that all those who helped British in Saunders murder case, which is known as 'Lahore conspiracy case', were rewarded with cash, property and promotions in service. Hans Raj Vohra, Jai Gopal, P.N. Ghose and Manmohan Bannerji who deposed before court as approvers against Bhagat Singh and his comrades got these rewards. Jai Gopal got a cash award of Rs 20,000. P.N. Ghosh and Manmohan Banerji was recipient of 50 acres of land each in Champaran district of Bihar which was their home district. Though Vohra refused to take any monetary benefit but he was compensated by sending to England for higher studies in London School of Economics. After doing masters in political science, Vohra got a degree in journalism from London University. After this he worked as correspondent of the Civil and Military Gazette of Lahore till 1948. He later shifted to Washington and became Washington correspondent of a leading Hindi daily. Major P.D. Chopra who was jail superintendent was promoted to the rank of DIG. The then jail Deputy Superintendent, Khan Sahib Mohammad Akbar Khan, who could not withhold his tears after the execution of Bhagat Singh and his two comrades, was suspended but taken back as Assistant Jail Superintendent after some time. His title of 'Khan Sahib' was how ever withdrawn.

The investigation officer of Bhagt Singh's case, Khan Bahadur Sheikh Abdul Aziz, was given out of turn promotion as DIG three years later. His was the only example in 200 years of British rule when person who had joined as constable retired as DIG. His son Masood Aziz was appointed as deputy superintendent of police by nomination in November 1931 in the Punjab Police, he was also given 50 acres of land in Lyallpur. Sudershan Singh,

DSP who burnt the bodies of these martyrs was promoted as Additional Superintendent of police Kasur. Besides all these there was one Rai Sahib Pandit Sri Kishan. He was trial magistrate in this case, and then SDM Kasur at the time of execution. After execution of three revolutionaries, he was given an 'appreciation letter' by the governor. This way British government gave some kind of benefits to all those who supported them against Indian revolutionaries. But, after independence no one bothered to disclose their names to the nation. These people enjoyed the fruit of their loyalties to the British and the privileges of free India. They were never brought to books.

Bhagat Singh was projected as 'terrorist' by British. He was portrayed as a man who believed in violence, but truth is entirely different. He valued human life that is why the bomb he threw in Central Legislative Assembly did not harm anyone. He never advocated violence; otherwise the explosion could have killed numerous political leaders present in the Assembly Hall including Moti Lal Nehru, Madan Mohan Malviya and Mohammad Ali Jinnah and many more, if he had wanted so. The aim was just to awaken the British government about India's long pending demand of independence. He said: "It is famous that I am a terrorist but I am not that. I am a revolutionary who has certain ideology, defined ideals and a long programme and if people think that after living in for a long period in the jail, there is any change in my ideologies then they are wrong. It is my firm belief that we cannot get anything through bombs or pistols. Throwing bomb is not only dangerous but also harmful. It is required in certain specific conditions. Our main aim is the organization of labourers and farmers."

If we see today's scenario the things have not changed much. Labour and peasants are being exploited; foreign companies are welcomed to exploit our manpower and natural resources. These were the evils against which Bhagat Singh and his comrades fought. So in such conditions, Bhagat Singh is more relevant today. After, almost 68 years of independence common man does not feel free. The state is abdicating its responsibility of providing good living conditions to its masses. Instead private players are being involved in the process. The illegal activities of companies are being legitimized in the name of obstacle free capitalist economy, but demand of labourers for minimum wages and demand of small and medium farmers for subsistent support price for their produce in not being listened even. It was this fact, which had disturbed Bhagat Singh and his comrades. April 8th, 1929, the Lahore Assembly was to pass a bill, which could have nullified the rights of the trade unions and labours. And this was the occasion, he felt, and best, to convey his anger to those in powers. Bhagat Singh and his friends became immortal, the genuine voice of the common man, labourers and farmers of the country. While the bomb was not really meant to damage the assembly hall and kill political leaders as they had made their intentions very clear. They became revolutionaries who inspired the entire nation cutting across caste and communal lines. In fact, it is heartening that Bhagat Singh is still an icon for the youths all over the country.

Bhagat Singh was against the communalism. He ridiculed India's caste system and questioned the genuineness of a system, which make people untouchable on the basis of their birth in a particular caste. He was not oblivious of country's capitalist class, which was compromising with the British imperial community. It was his strong belief that this system based on exploitation cannot be eliminated with just transfer of power from the British to India. He wanted some fundamental economic changes in it.

Now country is facing same problems which Bhagat Singh had visualized eight decades back. In these conditions it seems imperative to find solution through the ideology of Bhagat Singh.

Manik Sarkar: Honesty incarnate

It is an irony that India the land of Gautam Buddha and Guru Nanak, has now become synonymous with corruption. The scandals and other financial irregularities are taking front page of daily newspapers. The moral values have gone down. Our leaders and bureaucrats have become epitome of corrupt practices. Almost every political leader is using public money for his personal needs. The exorbitant telephone bills of Haryana ministers are one very small example of it. The use of 'red beacon' on cars has become a fashion. There is no control over it.

An atmosphere has been created in the country that every citizen is corrupt and running after amassing wealth. They equate the corruption of our top leaders (some of whom are cooling their heels behind the bars), bureaucrats and businessmen with the corruption of bus conductors, lower division clerks, and labourers who at times shirk work. Unfortunately they are successful to some extent in this nefarious propaganda. That is why now corruption has taken back seat in elections. The elections of Lok Sabha and assembly elections in Punjab, Himachal Pradesh and Gujrat are glaring examples of it. In these states all the candidates, from any party or without party, who could just 'throw' money like anything, have won the election. This has become mindset of the people, and of some politicians too, that no one can win an election without money. This kind of general perception has disheartened the honest politicians. Such leaders and workers still exist in this world and in all the parties, though they are being sidelined systematically.

But, as truth always prevails, so does honesty. The elections of Tripura have proved it without any iota of doubt. Can any chief minister of any state match the honesty of Mr Manik Sarkar, the fourth time Chief Minister of this state where insurgency was the main problem? This man not only tackled this serious issue successfully but put the state on the path of development. Media which has been underplaying his work and 'honesty' since long is now compelled to trickle out some information about this 'man of honesty'.

Most of the readers will not believe the fact that the bank balance of this man decreased in his tenure as Chief Minister. Son of a tailor, he does not possess any moveable or immoveable property. An ancestral house in the village was transferred to his name after the death of his mother which he gave to his sister. He does not have car, and even a cell phone. Contrast this with Punjab where, leave alone Chief Minister even an ordinary Member of Legislative Assembly (MLA) or Bureaucrat move with a red beacon and gunmen. Above all, most of the political leaders who occupy government accommodation feel it 'humiliating' to vacate it even after they lose their official status to occupy the same. This is their moral character. The telephone bills of Haryana Ministers run in crores. How one can justify such hefty burden on state exchequer? On the contrary Manik Sarkar does not use even 'Red beacon' (light) on his official car.

His morning starts with washing of clothes. He donates his whole salary to his party [CPI (M)], and gets Rs 5000/- as subsistence allowance. He is a commerce graduate. Media has named him the 'poorest' Chief Minister but to me he is the 'richest man' as far as the unparallel support amongst 93% of Tripura voters is concerned. The people of the state have reposed full faith in his leadership with three- fourth majority. Under his able leadership Left Front has won 50 seats, (one more than the last elections) out of the total strength of 60 in Tripura assembly elections. So, the reins of this tiny, but very important state stays in the hands of Manik Sarkar. The leaders who instead of giving some solutions to the problems of common man such as - inflation, rapid price rise, suicide by farmers, unemployment, regularly increasing prices of petroleum products, use lousy language against each other just to divert the focus of the common man from the real problems. Such leaders should have the moral courage to learn some lesson from Manik Sarkar. They should not underestimate the intelligence of the voters. Their 'termite', 'Scorpio' and 'snake' like terminology and some other gimmicks can only fetch them some laughter and a few claps at a gathering, but not votes all the time. Such leaders who talk senseless can't find any solutions. Gujrat Chief Minister who called Congress a 'termite' is perhaps oblivious of the fact that every second child in his own state is suffering from malnutrition. It is the state where maximum smuggling of wine is taking place. Victims of 2002 riots still running from pillar to post to get justice, many of the refugees living in camps do not want to go back to their homes as they don't feel safe at their place.

They have been terrorized by the goons. Is it the 'development model' of Gujrat? Merely constructing huge Malls and a few roads in big cities do not make a state 'developed'. The safety of its citizens is the prime and the foremost duty of the state, if a Chief Minister fails to protect the lives of its people how he can save the people of the whole nation?

On the other hand Manik Sarkar is successful in bringing the insurgency down and makes people feel safe. In these conditions Manik Sarkar can be a role model for those who want to work with honesty. Is it not a ray of hope in this gloomy political scenario of the nation?

Devi Lal: A crusader of third alternative

Indian politics is on cross roads. Present government is losing its ground very fast; the question is who is next? The main opposition Congress is also not different from ruling alliance. Their economic policies are same. They both have no agenda for the poor. Their definition of development, progress, and prosperity is the economic growth of some individuals who can accumulate unaccounted wealth. Left parties could have been an automatic choice, but they are not strong enough for that. The emergence of third front seems a distant dream. Both Congress and BJP ridicule the idea of third force, because it would hamper their chances of swapping power. In these circumstances people have no option than to choose either of the two.

This reminds us the towering personality of Chaudhary Devi Lal, the man who produced third alternative very successfully. He was instrumental in bringing small parties together to form viable third political force. Today no one is as tall as Chaudhary Devi Lall was, so the emergence of third front is in jeopardy. Devi Lal was the crusader of the rights of farmers and other down trodden people of the country. Future generation would not believe that a politician of the largest democracy of the world let go the opportunity of becoming its Prime Minister, even after elected to it, because he was committed to upholding a promise made in public. At a time when greed was at its highest, he like a saint detached from the worldly temptations he turned away from power to set an unparalleled example in the country.

Chaudhary Devi Lal devoted almost 70 years to active politics. He is the only leader of modern history of the country, who put in power almost a dozen politicians. Of the three quarters of a century he spent in and out of power, he himself had the opportunity of availing only six years in power. He had a major role in installing four Prime Ministers, five Chief Ministers of joint Punjab, seven Chief Ministers of Haryana, three Chief Ministers of other states, seven Central Ministers and around six dozen Ministers of various states of the country. With the passage of time he was given the name of 'King Maker'. But he was not a 'king maker' like Chanakya. He was truly that kind of crusading leader for whom the corridor of power was never the goal. For him power was a tool for serving the people and never the object.

An interesting aspect of Devi Lal is that there is a curious mixture of the 'Ram Rajya' of Tulsi, the communism based on class consciousness and dialectic materialism of Karl Marx, Gandhism's Satyagraha and non- violence, the socialism of Acharya Narendra Dev and Lok Nayak Jai Parkash Narain, the non- Congressism of Dr. Ram Manohar Lohia and studied conclusions of the economist like Amartya Sen. The truth is that the seven decades of his life were so hectic that he neither had time nor the opportunity to give them a proper shape nor the intellectual around him took initiative to do so. Neither did this 'Marx' have an 'Engel' nor did he had the time and the inclination to himself put his thoughts in a proper order.

He lived his life on the principles of Marxism, Gandhism, Socialism and existentialism. He defined democracy in the simple language to make common man to understand it. He used to say, "Lok Raj Lok Laj se chalta hai" (democracy runs with humbleness). In the period after independence, from Dr. Gopi Chand Bhargava, Bhim Sen Sachar, Partap Singh Kairon to Bansi Lal, Bhajan Lal in the state and V.P. Singh and Chander Shekhar in the Centre he demonstrated time and again that he was not tempted by the desire to wield power. He truly crusaded for the stated objectives and values of life. By keeping himself away from the electoral battles of 1962,

1964, 1967 and 1968 he proved his sense of detachment. In his political career he contested 17 elections. Victory and defeat were same for him. He pursued certain values and the electoral politics was a tool and, therefore, of little importance.

Devi Lal always fought for the cause of peasants, working class and tenants. In the post independence Punjab he played a vital role in installing Dr. Gopi Chand Bharagva as Chief Minister, but, during the course of time Dr. Bharagva proved a wrong choice as he was pro- landlords. Those days Devi Lall was busy with the 'tenant- landlord' movement, so he had little interest in power politics. Since Dr. Bharagva was being partisan to landlords so it was imperative to change him. In fact the irony of Devi Lal's life began from this point onward when he was forced to wage battles against his own people and system. He launched a struggle against Bharagva and got success in removing Bharagva from the throne. On April 06, 1949 Bhim Sen Sachar became the Chief Minister of Punjab.

Devi Lal himself became the Chief Minister first on June 21, 1977 to June 1979 and second time from June 20, 1987 to December 02, 1989, but from Dr. Bharagva in joint Punjab to Omparakash Chautala, in contemporary times, his role in the election of Chief Minister has earned him the title of 'King Maker'. He played an important role in the election of Mahamaya Prasad Singh and Karpoori Thakur in Bihar, Charan Singh in Uttar Pradesh and Govind Narayn Singh in Madhya Pradesh as Chief Ministers. Later, the Prime Ministership of Charan Singh, V.P. Singh and Chander Shekhar were entirely the result of the efforts and initiative of Devi Lal.

Today when the need of the third front is felt badly, the tall personality like Devi Lal is missing. Had he been there the things could have been different. It is the difference which a man like 'him' can make.

Features

The Wobbling Fourth Pillar

Press or the media has the privilege to be called the fourth pillar of the democracy. All newsmen enjoy this status. The respect which people give to the 'pen' is immense. This is all due to the work of our predecessors, for whom journalism was a mission. They never compromised on principles, and hid the truth for money. They had the courage to call 'a spade, a spade'. It is their legacy which we are carrying forward. But are we honest? This is a big question mark in front of us. Common man in street has started looking at pressmen with a different eye. They see us with suspicion. They do not feel comfortable or safe in giving us the lead. Unfortunately, many of journalists who do not possess right aptitude for this profession are helm of affair in most of the media organizations, because such mediocrity suits the owners. These mediocre professionals work like puppets in hands of owners. They write, show or say what owner wants. For such people ethics of journalism have no meaning. In fact they work as 'yes man'. This is really frustrating for the right kind of persons.

There was a time when editors used to be the backbone of the newspapers. A newspaper was known by the editor, but the trend has changed. Now the office of the editor has almost gone. Owners of the newspapers have themselves become editors. They want to keep the reins of the organization in their own hands to use it for their business interests. If we look around we find most of the newspapers, news magazines, periodicals, journals, and TV channels are owned either by big business houses, politicians or multinational companies. This is a great threat, not only to media world but to our democratic system too. Now the common man is no longer is the focus of our reporting. The fourth estate has become insensitive to the plight, agony and grief of the poor. That is why the suicides by farmers hardly find any space on front page in national newspapers. Most of such cases go unreported, what is reported, it is the point of view, story or version of government officials only, which they provide to the reporters. It is easy to file reports on these suicides from air conditioned chambers or offices, but very difficult to report the matter from the spot. Which reporter goes to these areas to have first hand information?

A very few of us will be aware of the fact that in the past 15 years more than 2, 00,000 farmers have committed suicide. Millions of farmers continue to live in perpetual indebtedness. According to Crime Record Bureau 17, 368 farmers had killed themselves in 2009, an increase of 7 percent over 2008 count. India is facing a thousand mutinies. Pitched battles are being fought across the country by poor farmers, who fear further marginalization when their land is literally grabbed by the government and industry. If we see from Manglore in Karnatka to Aligarh in Utter Pradesh, from Singur in West Bengal to Mansa in Punjab the whole India is boiling. Large chunks of agriculture land are being forcibly diverted for non agricultural purposes. Such news reports do not find much space in newspapers. No TV channel ever covers it in its right spirit because they don't find any sponsors for such stories. No debate or discussion is seen on TV screens on such topics.

Under these circumstances the role of dedicated and sincere journalists become crucial. It is true that the task is not easy. On one hand they are to fight 'pseudo' journalists and the might of multinationals on the other. The pressure of different political parties is another impediment in their way. These political outfits try to allure journalists by giving them many concessions. Unfortunately, a big lot of journalists easily fall prey to such lucrative offers. So this profession is losing its grace, and the sanctity. It is the responsibility of all the right thinking media men to fight this menace with strong will and iron hand, otherwise this wobbling 'fourth pillar' will one day fall crashing on our own heads.

This is Malls v/s Slums

No day passes when there is no scam unearth. People are becoming immune to these types of scams. They have accepted it, as they have accepted inflation, price rise, lawlessness, corruption and many other such evils. The big houses, corporate houses, multinationals and politicians are successful in convincing the people that corruption is a universal phenomenon, and if you pay some extra money for your work to be done, then what's the harm in it. Big houses pay commission for their deals. They consider it legitimate. Bofors gun deal is the living example before us. According to these elements, a person who works for you deserves to be compensated. At least he has got your work done. The second myth which they disseminate among masses is that everyone on this earth is corrupt. For them Mahatama Gandhi to Sardar Bhagat Singh, everyone was corrupt.

This is the typical character of capitalist economy. We shall have to understand that no private entrepreneur setup his project for the welfare of the people. His sole aim is to earn maximum profit and cumulate as much wealth as he could. Bearing the mask of 'welfare' is his compulsion. For earning money he can go to any extent. He is not scared of using fair or unfair means to achieve his goal. What to talk of giving other benefits, he is even shy of giving minimum wages to his employees. If they demand for that, they are shown the door. The labour laws in our country are such which do not help the worker at all. They are all practically pro industrialists. A daily wage worker can not fight legal battle in courts for years together. Then he is left with no other choice than to fight by some other means. Then he is not concerned whether these means are legal or illegal. In those conditions he can kill someone or get killed.

Same is the case with peasantry, there is hardly any day passes when no farmer commits suicide. According to reports more then 2, 00,000 farmers have committed suicides in the last 15 years. These figures show the real picture and gravity of situation. But government is trying to keep this very serious issue under the carpet. The figure of GDP and inflation which government give, do not convince the poor who is spending more money everyday for the products of his daily needs. He is not concerned what US President Brack Obama says about India or how our Prime Minister addresses Obama. They are also not concerned about the comments of big capitalists of the world about our country. He has no interest in 'Ambanies' or 'Lakshmi Mittales'. His only worry is about his morsel, his worry is about the education of his wards, his concern is about the medicines for his ailing father, his concern is about the marriage of his daughter and his anxiety is about the safety of his life. He wants to live a peaceful and smooth life, but the rat race in which this economic system has put us all, does not allow a worry less life. Just to make a few people billionaires our system is jeopardizing the future of the rest.

The Naxalite crisis in the country is the result of this economic and political disparity. More over government is treating and trying to solve it as a law and order problem, which has proved wrong. With police pressure it may subsides but resurfaces after some time. This is happening since 1967 or so. It is true that they are creating 'law and order problem' but its root cause is some where else. That is why the best efforts of the successive governments in this regard proved futile. In fact all such problems are the babies of our economic system, which erects shopping malls on one hand and slums on the other. If this process continues unabated the day is not far when these slums will 'encroach' upon the 'malls'.

Age is only numbers

One of my friends always says that 'age is only numbers'. He means that one should not get depressed by growing age. I think he is very right. Age is a feeling nothing else. It can be good news for those who work very hard to hide their age. When we see on the track or play fields, the grey hair people galloping pass the black haired youth, then the 'guilt' of having grey hair vanishes. Many athletes have proved that they can do better in their fifties or sixties.

Usain Bolt is a big name in world athletics. He surprised everyone by clocking 09.63 seconds for 100 meter dash. But, what would you say about the man of 60 plus who clocked 11.83 seconds just 2.20 second slower than Bolt? Besides this a 95 year Brazilian Frederio Fischer completed this distance in 20.41 seconds. Same is the story of women runners. Here 60 year old Polish lady Eva Bartosik clocked 14.23 seconds only 04.60 second slower than Bolt. 90 year old Huang Qiu (Taipei) encourages young runners by completing this race in 29.93 seconds.

These athletes have proved that the will to compete, surmounts all the physical and mental barriers a person has. Ours is a country where sports never took the front seat. It has always been a past time activity. That is why we are lagging behind in every sphere of life. We have the most of diabetic and heart patients in our country. We have created such an atmosphere in our society that a person completing 35 years of age is not fit for athletics, hockey, foot ball, badminton, wrestling, boxing and many more such games which requires real stamina, strength and endurance. They have been advised either to play indoor games like snooker, billiard, chess, or outdoor game like golf or some time cricket. No need to say that in a country where most of the people live below poverty line, except for a few from elite class, can afford these indoor or outdoor games. The result is obvious and we have maximum number of heart patients and diabetics. The number of people suffering from osteoarthritis and high blood pressure is very high. Every second person is suffering from back pain, disk dislocation or cervical spondylitis. These problems are more related to our modern life style than to anything else. The solution is simple- 'go and play' the games which really make you sweat, not the one which gives you enough time for discussing your office or business problems or allow to gossip or take sips of beer in between. Our newly introduced education system is also discouraging students to take physical activities. Parents are obsessed with marks, grades and divisions. They do not allow their wards to participate in outdoor activities. That is why the regular PT which once was the integral part of school curriculum is completely missing. Parents do not understand the repercussions of disassociating their kids from physical activities. Such youngsters easily get all sorts of medical problems.

We also don't feel ashamed on the fact that very small and under develop countries like Ethiopia, Uganda and Kenya get more medals than us in Olympic and other international competitions. If we talk of 2012 London Olympics, we find that an unknown athlete Stephan Kipratich from Uganda won the prestigious Marathon in 02:08.01 hours where as our runner Ram Singh Yadav finished poor 78th clocking 02:30.06 hours almost 22 minutes slower than the winner. This is the time with which Yadav could not have won this race even 52 years back in Rome (1960). In Rome all time great barefooted Abebe Bikila of Ethiopia had clocked 02:15.16 hours, almost 15 minutes faster than Yadav.

On one hand we find our youngsters shy of sports and physical activities, on the other hand athletes taking part in Masters Category look more enthusiastic and focused. It is right that for such athletes it is not easy to maintain their stamina and strength, but they are brave enough to do that.

This way they remain fit and without ailments. It is tragedy of our country that play fields give a deserted look and hospitals are overcrowded, where as it should have been other way around. Veteran athletes work really hard that is why they take themselves close to their young competitors. If we take the case of 1500 meter race in London Olympic Games, Algeria's Taoufik Makhloufi won the gold in 03:34.08 minutes, where as a veteran (35+) Bernard Lagat of US took 03:34.63 minutes, just 0.55 seconds slower than Makhloufi for the same distance at New York in June 2012. In fact he was better than the second finished Leonel Manzano of US who clocked 03:34.79 minutes. Another US runner Nolan Shaheed in 60+ categories, covered this distance in 04:32.97 minutes. In women section Yunxia Qu of China has a record of 03:50.46 minutes, which she established in 1993. A veteran athlete (35+) Tatyana Tomashova of Russia has completed this distance in 03:59.71 minutes.

I want to say that these oldies are not far behind rather they are very close on the heels of their young friends. The victory for young ones cannot be granted. Let us see when 'Old becomes Gold'

Printed in the United States
By Bookmasters